"Nicole Castleton, I have a confession to make."

What was going on?

As Miguel dropped to one knee beside her, he reached into the lapel of his jacket, pulled out a small velvet box and flipped open the lid, revealing a modestly sized but sparkling diamond.

"I let you get away from me once because I was young and afraid to fight for what I wanted. But I won't make that mistake again."

He let *her* get away?

"Will you marry me, Nicole? Will you be my wife, the mother of my children? Will you be my best friend, my lover, my partner for the rest of my life?"

Tears welled in her eyes, and emotion clogged her throat. At one time, she'd dreamed of a night like this one, hoped for a proposal like this. Yet as surreal, romantic and magical as this evening was, it had been bought and paid for. And that bittersweet reality made for a bride who was blushing and teary-eyed for all the wrong reasons.

Dear Reader,

If you're a fan of the Fortunes of Texas the way I am, you'll understand how happy I was to be asked to work on the 2013 series, The Fortunes of Texas: Southern Invasion. It's always fun to work with the other authors in creating a continuity series, but it's also nice to return to Red Rock and revisit some of the characters who have become real over the years.

This time, I had the opportunity to write the story of Miguel Mendoza and his high school sweetheart, Nicole Castleton. Ten years ago, Miguel and Nicole went through a devastating breakup, and Miguel left town to escape the heartbreak. Now he's a happy and successful sales exec for Home Run Records in New York.

But Nicole doesn't let the distance stop her when she's forced to find a husband—and fast! She's also prepared to offer Miguel a deal he can't refuse. Trouble is, the chemistry between them is even stronger than ever.

So find a cozy spot to sit back and enjoy another Red Rock romance.

Happy reading!

Judy

MARRY ME, MENDOZA!

JUDY DUARTE

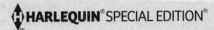

HARLEQUIN® SPECIAL EDITION®

Special thanks and acknowledgment to Judy Duarte
for her contribution to the
Fortunes of Texas: Southern Invasion continuity.

Recycling programs
for this product may
not exist in your area.

ISBN-13: 978-0-373-65735-3

MARRY ME, MENDOZA!

Printed in U.S.A.

Books by Judy Duarte

JUDY DUARTE

always knew there was a book inside her, but since English was her least favorite subject in school, she never considered herself a writer. An avid reader who enjoys a happy ending, Judy couldn't shake the dream of creating a book of her own.

Her dream became a reality in March 2002, when Silhouette Special Edition released her first book, *Cowboy Courage*. Since then she has published more than twenty novels. Her stories have touched the hearts of readers around the world. And in July 2005 Judy won a prestigious Readers' Choice Award for *The Rich Man's Son*.

Judy makes her home near the beach in Southern California. When she's not cooped up in her writing cave, she's spending time with her somewhat enormous but delightfully close family.

To the authors who worked on this series with me:
Allison Leigh, Susan Crosby, Marie Ferrarella,
Cindy Kirk and Crystal Green.
You made this book a pleasure to write.

Chapter One

Nicole Castleton's nerves were so tightly strung, her stomach so knotted, that she was just about to climb the walls of the exclusive Red Rock Country Club, where Marnie McCafferty's bridal shower was in full swing.

She ought to be thrilled that everything was going just as she'd planned—the decorations, the food, the service. Even the weather, which had been gray and drizzly yesterday, had turned sunny and bright for the happy occasion. But everything else in her life was about to blow sky-high, and she needed to confide in her best friend.

As the guests milled about, sipping champagne or mimosas, Nicole glanced at her bangle wristwatch. Now was her chance.

She crossed the room, pulled the soon-to-be blushing bride aside and lowered her voice to a whisper. "Marnie, I've got a big problem, and I need to talk to you—alone."

Marnie, who was going to marry Asher Fortune and become a mommy to his son, Jace, glanced at the guests, zeroing in on her future in-laws, the Atlanta Fortunes, as well as the Fortunes who called Red Rock home. Then she turned back to Nicole, her head cocked slightly. "You want to talk privately now?"

Nicole nodded. "Yes. Let's get out of here for a moment and find a place that's quiet."

As the two friends slipped off together, Nicole led the way to a side door that opened onto the patio.

When they were finally out of earshot, Marnie asked, "What's wrong?"

Nicole released a sigh before blurting out the dilemma she'd been dealing with ever since her parents had dropped the bomb on her two days ago. "I need to get married—and fast!"

The I-couldn't-be-happier glow Marnie had been wearing ever since Asher Fortune had popped the question faded, and her brow furrowed. "Oh, no. Are you *pregnant?*"

As wild and impossible as that sounded, a pregnancy might actually make things easier—in a way. But Marnie had connected all the wrong dots. "Of course not. I'm not even *dating* anyone. You know that."

"I'm sorry. It was the first thing that came to mind when you mentioned having a problem that marriage would solve. So let's slow down and take a step back.

Why on earth would you need to get married? Are you in some kind of trouble?"

Nicole was in trouble all right. "I stand to lose everything I ever wanted in life—Castleton Boots."

"I don't understand." Marnie tucked a long strand of light brown hair behind her ear. "It's a booming company. At least, the few shares of stock I own are doing well. And you're the sole heir."

"That's what I'd always thought."

"What happened?"

"Bottom line?" Nicole crossed her arms. "I'm being blackmailed by my manipulative parents."

"That doesn't make any sense. Your parents adore you and always have."

There was no arguing that. Nicole had been a "miracle baby," born late in life, when her parents had all but given up on having a child. So needless to say, they'd lavished her with material possessions as well as unconditional love. But apparently, they'd changed their minds and included a few "conditions" on their affections.

"They're holding Castleton Boots for ransom," Nicole explained. "They'd always said they would pass the company on to me when they retired, but apparently there are strings attached. I can't inherit the company unless I'm married."

"But that's crazy. And so unfair."

"My thoughts exactly." The family-owned company manufactured beautifully crafted cowboy boots frequently seen on the red carpet in Hollywood and on the country-western tour circuit, and the stock in question was worth a fortune. But that was beside the point.

Nicole had gone to work for the family business right out of college, but nothing had been given to her. She'd started at the bottom as a receptionist and had moved up the ranks to vice president—and all on her own merits. Her father might spoil her in other ways, but no one got a free ride at Castleton Boots.

"Maybe they're bluffing," Marnie said.

"That's what I'd hoped. So I went to an attorney— my own, not the corporate firm. And it's legit."

Marnie paused a beat, her brow furrowed.

"You know how I feel about Castleton Boots," Nicole added. "That company is my life. I've worked my tail off to prove that I'm not just a pretty face or the CEO's daughter. And I refuse to stand by and watch them sell the business to strangers."

"So what are you going to do?"

"The only thing I can do—play by their rules. And that means I need to get married—ASAP."

"But how do you plan to pull that off? You've been so focused on work that you haven't dated anyone in ages—that is, unless you met someone in the past couple days and didn't tell me about him."

Nicole chuffed. "Yeah, right. Who has time to date? And even if I decided to make the time and take that route, it would take forever to find the right someone. And I don't want to wait on chance. I've devoted my entire life to the company, and now Dad has some chronic health problems, so he's ready to hand the reins over to someone else—anyone but me, it seems."

"Wow. Castleton Boots has been in your family for generations. You think they'd really sell it?"

"Apparently so. But that's not even the real issue here. They're afraid that they're running out of time to become grandparents, and they're trying to force me into finding a husband." Nicole blew out another sigh. "I'm so tired of my parents trying to control my life."

"Well, you can't just snag the first man who comes along and ask him to marry you."

"No, maybe not. But I have to do something. And if their little manipulation scheme backfires on them, then that's too bad. It would serve them right."

Marnie reached for Nicole's upper arm. "You're not thinking about arranging some sort of marriage of convenience to appease your parents, are you?"

"To be honest? That was my first thought. But if I came home this weekend and claimed to have met Mr. Right, it would be pretty obvious to them that the relationship was a fake. Trouble is, I have no idea where I'd find a husband fast. It's not like I can just force myself to fall in love. After all, I'd never be able to plan something like that. Love just…"

Her speech drifted off, as memories of her teenage romance with Miguel Mendoza came to mind.

Back then, her life had revolved around her studies, cheerleading and weekends riding horses and talking about boys with Marnie. But one day, her biology teacher had assigned Miguel to her study group, hoping the laid-back teen would learn a few good work habits.

The teacher, who'd also been the varsity baseball coach, had said as much when he'd introduced him to Nicole's group. "Mendoza, you need help with your study skills. And who better to show you the ropes than the top students at Red Rock High?"

Nicole hadn't been sure how adding the D student to her group would work out, since the gorgeous dark-haired boy had been labeled trouble by more than one teacher. But Miguel hadn't been a bad kid. He just enjoyed having a good time and making his friends and classmates laugh.

And to be honest, Nicole had found him just as entertaining as anyone.

After Mr. Marquez had walked away, leaving Miguel behind, Nicole had said, "Take a seat, Mendoza."

After that, Paco Ramirez and Lena Hsu had followed her lead, referring to him by his last name. But it hadn't taken the two science nerds very long to complain that Mendoza wasn't pulling his own weight.

But Nicole had begun to realize that wasn't the case. Miguel was actually struggling academically, and his goofing off wasn't because he didn't want to do the work but because he *couldn't*. Much of his wisecracking, sweet-talking personality was a front, and hidden inside there was a really good and deeply insecure person.

So she had taken him aside and offered to work with

him one-on-one. And before that semester had ended, they had fallen in love.

As if reading her mind, Marnie eased closer. "Nicole, are you thinking about Miguel?"

Nicole would have denied it if her best friend didn't know her so well. "I admit that he momentarily crossed my mind."

Okay, so invaded her mind was more like it. That stylishly mussed dark hair, those playful brown eyes, that dazzling smile...

Back in the day, she'd imagined herself head-over-heels in love with Miguel, but what did a seventeen-year-old girl know about things like forever and lifetime commitments?

"You'd better cross Miguel Mendoza off your list of potential fake husbands," Marnie said. "Even if he still lived in Red Rock and agreed to your plan, it would never work. Your parents would not only freak out if you brought him home and told them he was the one, they'd probably cut you out of the will completely."

Ten years ago, when Nicole's parents had learned that their Ivy League college-bound honor student had fallen for a young man who was practically flunking out of school, they'd thrown a walleyed fit, claiming she was dating beneath her.

Not that Miguel had been born on the wrong side of the tracks by any means. He'd grown up in a respectable, middle-class family. But the Castletons still felt he wasn't good enough for the daughter they considered a Texas princess.

So telling her parents that the two of them had reconnected and had decided to renew their romance would go over like a swarm of bees in a space suit.

But then again, for that very reason, telling them she'd reconnected with Miguel would certainly be believable, based upon how badly she'd felt following their breakup, how worried her parents had been about her.

But why wouldn't she have felt badly? Miguel had all but disappeared off the face of the earth after the night they'd split up. And even if she'd wanted to backpedal and tell him to hang in there, the Mendozas had gone to a family reunion at a beachfront hotel on the Yucatan Peninsula the following week. And when they returned to Red Rock, Miguel wasn't with them.

From what she'd heard, he'd stayed with his uncle and finished school in Mexico, eventually returning to the states and landing a job in New York City.

Nicole hadn't even seen him since the night they'd broken up, the night he'd held her in his arms one last time and told her he'd always be there for her, that if she ever needed him, he'd drop everything and…

And *there* was the solution to her problem. The only solution, really, considering her parents' demand and the ticking clock.

"Uh-oh." Marnie grabbed Nicole's arm. "I can practically see those cogs turning in your brain. What are you plotting?"

"A plan so wild that it just might work." As a slow smile spread across Nicole's face, her mood lifted. "Rather than trying to conjure up a believable fiancé and spin a yarn about how we fell in love at first sight, I can tell them I'm marrying for love—and they won't be able to dispute it."

"What are you talking about?" Marnie asked, arching a brow.

"I'm going to marry Miguel Mendoza."

"You've got to be kidding."

"Not at all. It's the only way out—and it's perfect. I'll get my company by following the letter of the law. The attorney assured me that the document doesn't put any restrictions on *who* I can marry, only that the marriage has to be legitimate."

All she had to do was get Miguel to agree to a limited marriage of convenience. She'd pay him handsomely for his time, of course. All he had to do was act as if he was still in love with her.

"Assuming that Miguel would even go along with something that wacky," Marnie said, "you'd have to find him first. And what if he's married or seriously involved with someone?"

"Actually, I know right where to find him. He works for a record company in New York City. And he's *not* married or seriously involved."

"How do you know?"

"Because I kept tabs on him over the past ten years through the Red Rock grapevine."

The real question was, would she be able to convince Miguel to go along with her plan? He'd definitely moved on with his life, but had he forgotten what they'd once felt for each other?

Would he honor the promise he'd made her?

Or would he think the whole thing was stupid?

"Listen," Marnie said, "I really have to get back to my guests. We can talk more about this later."

"Of course." Talk about cogs spinning, Nicole's mind had slipped into overdrive with all she needed to do to put her plan in action. "I'll be right behind you, Marnie. Just give me a minute."

After her friend went back to the country club garden room, where the white-linen-draped tables had been adorned with crystal rose bowls holding lush red blooms, Nicole lingered on the patio a moment longer, feeling better than she had in days. She finally had an amazing solution to her problem.

She would fly to New York tomorrow and present the offer to Miguel in person at Home Run Records, where he worked.

He might not be up for the ruse, but there was one thing to be said about Miguel. He was an honorable man. And she had every intention of reminding him of the very last thing he'd said to her, the promise he'd made her.

If you ever need me, all you have to do is say the word. And I'll be there for you.

Well, the day had come when Nicole needed Miguel. And she needed him *now.*

Locked away in his office at Home Run Records, Miguel Mendoza sat back in his desk chair and stretched, arching his cramped shoulders and back.

He'd been scanning sales reports and making notes all morning, preparing for a meeting with the marketing department. Company profits had dropped over the last quarter, and it was up to him to lay out a plan to turn things around.

He was an ace at problem solving and had already come up with a few ideas. In fact, that's why the CEO had come to him days ago and offered him a promotion if he'd take a desk job.

But Miguel hated being confined to an office. As a sales exec, he ran a lot of PR events across the country and rarely stayed in one place for very long. The fast pace kept things interesting for him, if not exciting. So that's why he'd turned down the promotion, even if it would have helped him sock away more money for the nightclub he planned to open someday.

He rolled his chair back from the desk and got to his feet. For some reason, being cooped up behind four walls bothered him more today than usual, and he was eager to get that meeting out of the way and to take off for the rest of the day.

Outside, on the city street, several horns blared. Most New Yorkers ignored the common sound, but Miguel, who'd been prone to distraction, especially in school, made his way to the window and spotted a stalled vehicle in the intersection below. For a moment, he watched the midday traffic, the rush of people making their way to and from the subway station.

Manhattan was a far cry from Red Rock, Texas. And while he missed his family, the move to the Big Apple had been a good one for him. It had given him an opportunity to connect with people in the music industry, as well as those who had successful nightclubs who'd be happy to advise him when the day came.

His stomach growled, reminding him he hadn't eaten much this morning, just black coffee and a muffin from the Starbucks on the corner. He'd probably be a lot more focused if he put some protein in his system.

He glanced at the clock. It was nearly noon, but he didn't have time for a real break. He'd probably have to order a sandwich from the deli on the corner. But before he could make a move, the intercom buzzed, drawing him back to his desk, back to work.

He picked up the phone and hit the button that would allow his secretary's call through. "Yes, Margo."

"There's a woman here to see you."

Miguel glanced at the calendar on his iPhone. Had he scheduled an appointment and forgotten it?

No, he just had that departmental meeting at two.

Good thing, too, because he didn't have time for any mental detours right now.

"Who is she?" he asked.

"She says she's an old friend—Nicole Castleton?"

Miguel's gut clenched. Nicole was in New York? At Home Run Records?

To say he was surprised would be an understatement. And for a man who was quick on his feet, who always had a ready response, he couldn't quite find one.

He raked his fingers through his hair, then said, "Send her in, Margo."

While waiting for Nicole's entrance, he probably should have taken a seat at the desk, pretending that she'd caught him hard at work instead of on a break, but he remained on his feet until the door swung open and the tall, shapely brunette stepped into the room.

He'd been reminded of her every time he spotted Kate Middleton, the future queen of England, on the cover of a magazine. And just the sight of the real Nicole now, a debutante all grown up, set his pulse racing.

But damn. She'd been stunning at seventeen and a bit on the slender side, but in the last ten years, she'd grown even lovelier, filling out in all the right places.

"I probably should have called to let you know I was in town, but I was afraid you might not see me. So I thought I'd just stop by," she said. "I hope you don't mind me surprising you like this."

Mind? Her arrival had completely blindsided him, to say the least. And he'd be damned if he knew what to think or how to respond, let alone how he felt about it.

Wearing a classic black dress and killer heels, she looked like any successful New York exec. And while she'd fit right in on the streets of Fifth Avenue, there'd always be a bit of Red Rock in her.

At that thought, a bit of the tension eased, and he said, "I like surprises. Always have."

She wore her hair longer now. And those silky strands might even be glossier than before.

"What brings you to New York?" he asked.

Nicole merely stood there for a moment, staring at him as if she couldn't remember why she'd come. Finally, she said, "I flew in for a meeting. I won't be here long, but I thought I'd…" She scanned his office, her gaze landing back on him, setting off an adolescent buzz through his bloodstream. "Well, I thought I'd stop by and say hello. It's been a long time."

Ten years, to be exact.

A lifetime ago.

A flood of memories rushed back, threatening to sweep him off his feet.

Holding hands under the table in study hall. Slipping behind the dugout for a kiss. Steaming up the windows of his brother's car while parked at that construction site overlooking downtown Red Rock…

Miguel had fallen hard for Nicole back then, only to have her jerk the rug out from under his feet when she'd told him she couldn't see him anymore.

She'd needed to focus on her studies, she'd explained. She'd had plans to attend a private college that required community service projects, as well as good grades, and she'd needed to get that under way. In a way, he'd supposed that was true. But he'd always known there was more to it than that. Her parents, particularly her father, hadn't liked her dating anyone in high school, especially a guy they'd thought was beneath her. And she'd buckled to their demands.

Yet in spite of it all—the heartbreak and disappointment, the resentment that had grown over time—her presence alone sent his body into overdrive.

But he couldn't very well stand here gawking at her

like a love-struck teen, so he pointed to one of the chairs in front of his desk. "Come on in. Have a seat."

She complied, and he followed suit, sitting across from her.

"Nice office," she said, as she scanned the room.

An awkward silence filled the air, threatening to choke the breath right out of him.

Or was that just the result of the sexual attraction that had always sparked every cell in his being whenever he caught sight of Nicole?

He wished he could say that he hadn't given her any thought since their breakup, but that wasn't true. In spite of himself, she'd become some kind of benchmark for every woman he dated. And in recent years, he'd gone out with more than his fair share.

Nicole.

Here.

Now.

Another swirl of youthful memories bombarded him, and while he did his best to shake them off, it was damn near impossible to do with her seated just steps away, a walking, talking teen goddess come back to earth for who knew what reason.

Goddess or ghost?

He couldn't be sure, but he couldn't very well continue to stare at her as if his brains had left town.

"I was sorry to hear about your mother," she said. "I know how much you loved her."

Miguel's mom had died unexpectedly of pneumonia

nearly three years ago, and it had been a blow to the entire family. A loss he still felt.

"Yeah. It was tough. Thanks." Miguel had never been sure what to say when people had offered their condolences, and this time was no different. Or maybe, coming from Nicole, it threw him off all the more.

"So," he said, struggling to find something to say for the first time in his life, "how are things going back in Red Rock?"

"It's…" She smiled, but it didn't reach those pretty brown eyes. "Everything is…good. Great."

No, it wasn't. Her cheeks bore a liar's flush as she glanced across the room toward the window—avoiding eye contact it seemed.

Lying had never come easy for Nicole, who'd always been as honest as the day was long. And Miguel had no reason to believe that time had changed that.

So why was she here?

Her explanation, that she just happened to be in New York and had decided to look him up, didn't ring true.

Not after their history.

Something was up, something that had brought her to him after all these years.

He had no idea what it might be, but life back in Red Rock wasn't nearly as picture-book-perfect as she might have implied. And he'd bet his new Bose headphones that she hadn't just stopped by Home Run Records for old times' sake.

She'd gone to the trouble of looking him up, doing

her homework, just like the honor student she used to be.

And while he had to admit he was a bit flattered by her efforts to find him, curiosity trumped flattery.

What brought her to his office?

In the past ten years, there'd been plenty of opportunities for the two of them to run into each other—if they'd had a mind to. He'd made quite a few trips back to Red Rock to see his family, especially last spring, when his brother Javier had nearly died from injuries suffered in that tornado.

But Miguel had always made it a point not to go anywhere he might run into Nicole—or her parents.

And he figured she'd avoided his favorite hangouts during the holidays, as well.

"Okay," he said, "what's up? You didn't just stop by to say hello."

She blew out a sigh. "You're right. I flew to New York for just one purpose—to see you."

Her honesty nearly knocked him out of his chair, although he wasn't sure why it would. Maybe it was his skepticism doing that. After all, he'd been home at Christmas. She could have found a way to see him then, if she'd really wanted to.

Why here?

Why now?

"This is much harder than I thought it would be," she said.

What in the world had she come to say?

His mind, which had always been creative, went off

on a tangent, scampering to figure out why she'd come all this way and what made it so difficult to spill the beans.

Oh, God. His heart dropped to his gut. Had she come to tell him about a love child they'd had?

If so, waiting ten years after the fact was enough to fire up his temper.

But then again, he doubted that she would have been able to keep a secret like that. Red Rock wasn't that big of a town. Besides, he had a big family—Luis, his father, as well as his brothers, Rafe, Marcos and Javier, and his half sister, Isabella. On top of that, two of his siblings had married into the Fortune family—Marcos, who'd married Wendy, and Isabella, who'd married J.R.

Word of a love child would have gotten out.

So what else could it be?

Had she come to tell him that she'd never stopped loving him? That she regretted not standing up to her parents when they'd insisted she break up with him?

If so, that fired him up, too. Who buried feelings like that for ten whole years?

Either way, whatever it was, he was all ears.

And she was as quiet as the proverbial church mouse.

Finally, he said, "Why don't you just spit it out, Nic."

She glanced at the clasped hands in her lap, then back at him. "Okay, Miguel. Here's the deal. I've worked my butt off at Castleton Boots, and I assumed that I'd inherit it one day—not just because I was an only child, but because my efforts would be rewarded. But apparently, my parents have a legal stipulation that forces me to marry in order to take control of the company."

Miguel wasn't sure what she was getting at or where she was going with all of this. "I don't understand."

"If I don't get married within the next month, my parents will sell the company."

"So what does that have to do with me?"

Nicole bit down on her bottom lip, clearly pondering her answer. About the time Miguel suspected she'd take her response to the grave, she said, "I need you to help me show my parents that they can't run my life anymore."

He had a creative mind, but he still wasn't following her. "How in the world do you expect me to do that?"

She drew up straight, her hands gripping the padded armrest, and leaned forward, those pretty brown eyes zeroed in on his. "Marry me, Mendoza."

Chapter Two

Marry her?

Was she kidding? That was insane.

Miguel sat back in his desk chair, trying to make sense of it all.

Whatever wild-ass assumptions he'd made about her reasons for coming to see him had been wrong. There was no secret baby—thank goodness. No heartfelt apologies for not standing up to her parents' unfair demands. No ten-years-too-late professions of love.

Apparently, she'd just wanted to use him to dupe her parents.

The whole idea blew him away. Did she actually think he'd agree to it?

Yet for some crazy reason, the scheme intrigued him, too.

"Why me?" he asked. "I'd think that most of the single men in Red Rock would line up to help you out, especially if it meant a little hand-holding and a public kiss or two."

"First of all, I'm talking a real marriage—with a divorce down the road, of course. And secondly, my parents would never believe that I'd suddenly fallen in love with someone I'd never even dated before. They'd know it was only a marriage of convenience from the get-go. And since you and I were romantically involved and loved each other once upon a time, they'd be more apt to believe the marriage was the real deal."

She'd certainly gotten the "once upon a time" right. And while Miguel wanted to tell the Castletons' little princess that she'd wasted the good part of her day, as well as the cost of a first-class airline ticket, he gave her offer more consideration than he probably should.

If truth be told, he might be annoyed by her marriage plan, yet he was slightly flattered by it at the same time.

"I'm sorry," she said, releasing a soft sigh and sitting back in her seat. "This isn't coming out the way I'd wanted it to."

He wasn't sure she could have expressed it any better. She was asking him to marry her. But only as a means to trick her parents into handing Castleton Boots over to her.

It was the most outrageous thing he'd ever heard. Yet it was also very tempting.

And for more reasons than one. Not only would he get a chance to know the adult Nicole a little better, but the Castletons would get a little payback for what they'd stolen from him.

What he wouldn't give to see the looks on their faces when they learned their little princess was going to marry the grown-up kid they'd thought wasn't good enough for her.

Of course, knowing them, they'd feel that way about almost anyone Nicole might date. They'd always expected her to marry a doctor, lawyer or stockbroker— certainly not a successful PR whiz who'd always dreamed of opening up his own nightclub.

But as bitter as Miguel might be about the past, he'd moved on. He wasn't that same enamored teenager who couldn't look beyond a tall, long-haired beauty with big brown eyes anymore.

Besides, he wasn't about to walk away from his job at Home Run Records just for the opportunity to screw over the Castletons.

Or would he?

As irresponsible and reckless as it might be, he'd sure like a chance to even the score.

"Okay, Nicole. Let's say I did go along with your little marriage plan. What's in it for me?"

"I'd pay you. And very well." She tucked a strand of hair behind her ear, revealing a whopping pair of diamond studs and a swanlike neck made for a trail of kisses.

The money wasn't nearly as tempting as she was, assuming that she planned for them to be phony spouses with benefits. Talk about tempting…

"Do you still want to open that nightclub?" she asked.

Miguel drew up in his seat. That had been a dream of his ever since his family had made their first trip to his uncle's resort on the Yucatan Peninsula. And it helped to know that Nicole hadn't forgotten some of the things he'd told her.

"Don't look so surprised," she said. "I remember every conversation we ever had, Miguel—especially the last one."

The night she'd broken up with him? The moon-lit summer night his teenage world had come crashing down on him because she'd refused to stand up to her parents?

"Do you remember the last thing you said to me?" she asked. "You told me you'd be there for me if I ever needed you."

He'd said that, all right. And he'd meant it.

"Well, I need you *now,* Miguel."

As their eyes met, as their gazes locked, the years rolled back, and they were seventeen again.

When she looked at him like that…

Damn her. And damn him for even considering the stupid offer for even a moment.

"Please say yes, Miguel."

He *couldn't.* There was no way he could go back to Red Rock with her—and not just because of his job.

"I'm sorry, Nicole. It won't work."

"Maybe not, but hear me out. Please give it some thought."

She was asking too much of him. Yet for some inexplicable reason, he wasn't quite ready to send her on her way just yet....

Okay, so he just wanted a chance to talk to her again, to see the changes ten years had made. And he had a meeting to attend.

"I'll tell you what," he said, "I'll think about it."

Relief washed over her pretty face, brightening her eyes, lightening her load.

Before he could backpedal or respond, his intercom buzzed.

Margo was probably going to remind him of that meeting with marketing at two o'clock, and he couldn't blame her for that. He still had a lot of work to do on that report and just a little while longer to do it.

Margo had also seen how pretty Nicole was, and it was no secret that Miguel sometimes had a weakness for the ladies.

What she didn't know—and Miguel had managed to keep hidden for the past ten years—was that he'd really only had a weakness for this particular woman.

"I hate to keep you from your work," Nicole said. "We can talk more later. Maybe over dinner. That is, if you don't already have plans."

He didn't have any big plans, other than having an after-meeting drink with his coworkers.

But Nicole's game plan—even though he'd already decided not to get involved—would require further discussion. At least, she'd see it that way.

So he said, "Sure. Where are you staying?"

"The Ritz Carlton on Central Park South."

Why didn't that surprise him?

"Okay, I'll meet you in the lobby at eight."

She stood, flashed him an appreciative smile, then left his office, her hips swaying as a natural movement to her gait. He watched until the door closed behind her, wondering what he was getting himself into.

And hoping he wouldn't live to regret it.

New York City offered every type of food under the sun, so Miguel could have taken Nicole anywhere for dinner. As it was, he chose a place owned by the brother of one of his coworkers, a small Venetian restaurant located near Central Park.

He'd only eaten there a couple times, but the food was great. And the decor, with its tile floors, pale yellow plastered walls and dark beams, had an old-world charm.

The evening had started out quiet and awkward. But with time, the conversation lightened, and the smiles came easily.

Now as they sat across a linen-draped table for two, finishing their meals, Miguel reached for the bottle of Chianti and refilled their wineglasses.

"Thank you," she said.

"My pleasure."

Who would have thought that he'd be dining with his old high school flame tonight? That they'd actually find things to talk about that didn't have anything to do with their painful breakup?

Of course, he'd made a point of keeping the topic of

their conversation on the friends and teachers they'd known way back when.

"Remember when Bill Wiggins ran for Associated Student Body President?" she asked.

Miguel smiled. The tall, lanky kid had campaigned as Cowboy Bill and had plastered posters all over the high school campus showing himself wearing a white Stetson and a badge. "Are you talking about the time he staged that mock robbery of the cafeteria during lunch?"

"Yes. When Bill rode up to the senior lawn on his horse, all decked out like a Western sheriff, and saved the day, I thought he had the election in the bag."

"It was a clever campaign," Miguel said. "I'm not sure how he lost."

"If I remember correctly, he came very close to winning." Nicole rested her arm on the table, as if she'd somehow shaken off the awkwardness they'd both felt from the time he'd met her in the hotel lobby and they'd walked a block to the restaurant.

It might have been the wine, he supposed, but he found himself relaxing in his seat and enjoying their time together.

If she'd been anyone else, he might have suggested that she come home with him, but they had too much history for that. And even though their chemistry was still strong after all these years, he knew how things would play out.

Besides, she'd only approached him with a business proposition—one he couldn't possibly agree to, no matter how tempting it might be.

"Do you remember the time Coach Marquez caught us behind the dugout after the game with the Ridgeville Rockets?" she asked.

He smiled at the reminder. She'd watched his baseball practice one day, and when it was over, they'd snuck behind the dugout for a kiss that turned so hot it had damn near set the bleachers on fire.

Would kissing her again spark that same flame?

At the thought that it might, he tensed. It had taken a long time to get over her. And he'd never been one to repeat past mistakes.

"I was afraid he'd turn us in and that we'd get suspended from school," she added.

"It was just a kiss," Miguel said, downplaying the fact that all their kisses had set their adolescent hormones pumping.

"Was it?"

No. He'd had a lot of kisses over the past few years, and none had ever compared. But he wasn't about to admit it.

Curiosity still plagued him, though. And he couldn't help wondering if she'd be up to sharing another one tonight—just for old times' sake.

Talk about playing with fire....

The waiter, who'd approached their table while they'd been deep in conversation and wallowing in old memories, cleared his throat. When they looked up at him, he grinned. "I hate to interrupt, but I wondered if you'd like to see the dessert menu."

"That's not necessary," Miguel said. "Just bring us that chocolate decadent cake—if you still offer it."

"Absolutely," the waiter said, "it's probably the best thing on the menu."

Miguel glanced across the table at Nicole, the tension waning again. "I assume you still love chocolate."

She brightened. "I do, but let's only get one serving. We can share it."

Some things never changed, he supposed. When they were teenagers, she'd always passed on things like French fries or dessert, then would ask to share his. He'd come to expect it then. And it had never bothered him. He'd actually liked the intimacy.

"Is this a special evening?" the waiter asked. "An anniversary maybe?"

"No," Nicole said, "we're just old friends."

A grin tugged at the waiter's lips. "You must have been *good* friends."

Was it that obvious?

Maybe so, but they hadn't ended up as good friends, and that fact brought Miguel back to reality, back to their painful breakup.

As the waiter removed their dinner plates, he said, "I'll be back with your dessert."

After he left, Nicole leaned forward. "We *were* good friends, Miguel—the best ever. And I know that I'm asking a lot of you, but you're really the only one who can help me."

"It's not that easy. It's been ten years, and we've both moved on."

"I realize that. But I'll make it worth your time if you'll agree to help me."

Before taking the subway uptown to meet her, he'd actually considered it again, even though the whole idea was out of the question.

"Tell me something," he said. "Let's just say that you and I had run into each other accidentally today. And I'd asked you out to dinner—just for old times' sake. What would the chances be of us rekindling an old relationship?"

"It could happen."

"Really?"

His doubt was all too obvious and she grew silent, her brow furrowed as she studied the white linen tablecloth where her plate had once been. Then she looked back at him. "I know how badly you were hurt by our breakup. But don't forget, I was hurt, too."

He bristled. "Maybe so, but you were the one who rolled over and caved to your parents' demands."

"I was seventeen, Miguel. I had no other choice than to abide by their wishes."

So what? She'd ended it all as if none of what they'd shared, what they'd promised, what they'd planned, had meant anything. And after she'd walked away, she'd never even looked back.

"Besides," she added, "it was hard to rebel against them back then. They'd waited so long to have a child that their lives revolved around me, and I hadn't wanted to hurt them. But at the time," she added, "I hadn't realized just how controlling my parents really were. Or that they'd never stop trying to run my life after I grew up. And I can't let them get away with it anymore."

Even if he wanted to help her out, even if he *could* take a leave of absence and return to Red Rock, he wasn't so sure if he ever wanted to lay eyes on Andy and Elizabeth Castleton again.

When they'd found out that their princess was dating a boy they thought was beneath her, they'd insisted that she quit seeing him. And she hadn't been strong enough to defy them or to even suggest that they take a break from each other until she was of age and could make her own decisions about who to date, who to love.

Yet maybe it was just as well that it had ended when it did. Because he'd always known their relationship had been too good to last. Still, their breakup had hurt. And it had changed him—and his outlook on life—in a lot of ways.

For a while, he'd held out hope that they would get back together, but as the weeks wore on, it was clear that they were through. And each day they spent apart, his heart had shrunk a little more until he felt there was nothing left of him at all.

Fortunately, that summer he'd gone to a family reunion at Suenos del Sol, the beach resort in the Yucatan Peninsula his *tio* Pepe owned and operated. His mother's brother had always been one of Miguel's favorite relatives, so the timing had been perfect. There, on the white sandy beach, with the balmy tropical breeze tousling his hair and the sun on his face, he'd finally realized he would get over her eventually—as long as he didn't have to return to Red Rock and see her again. So he'd convinced his parents to let him finish out the school year in Mexico.

But as the summer passed, his heartache had turned to anger—at her for being weak, at her parents for being unfair and at fate for bringing them together only to tear them apart.

Yet here she was again.

I need you, she'd said.

There was a time when those words meant something very different. But she and her parents were playing games with each other, and he didn't want to be a part of it.

"I'm prepared to pay you a hundred thousand dollars."

She'd said she'd pay him well, but he'd had no idea she'd meant that much. And while tempted, the money somehow made it all the worse.

Miguel sat back in his seat. "I'm sorry, Nicole. I can't take you up on your offer—no matter how appealing it might be."

Her shoulders slumped slightly, and she nodded. "All right, I understand."

At that point, the waiter returned with the chocolate cake and set it in front of her, along with the two forks. But once they were alone again, she pushed the plate toward Miguel. "If you don't mind, I'm going to pass on dessert."

That was a first.

She scooted her chair back and stood. "Thank you

for meeting with me—and for dinner. It was delicious. If you'll excuse me, I'm going to walk back to the hotel. It's been a long day, and I'm exhausted."

So she was ending their evening together just like that? Accepting his decision without an argument, just as she'd done with her parents when they'd ordered her to stop seeing him?

Amazing, he thought. Yet wasn't that what he'd wanted her to do? Accept it and go back to Red Rock, leaving him here to continue living the life he'd created for himself?

He was happy in New York. Content.

His brothers always teased him about it, saying his life was one big kaleidoscope of wine, women and song. And while that was a stretch, part of it was true.

Miguel hadn't had a meaningful relationship since he and Nicole had broken up in high school. Of course, his travel schedule as a sales executive for the record company made it difficult to consider anything long-term with the women he dated. But he didn't have any complaints about that. Moving from city to city made his dating life interesting, too.

And it made the goodbyes easier for both parties.

But this parting was different, and he hoped he didn't live to regret it.

If there was one thing he learned this evening, somewhere deep inside, a tiny flame continued to burn for his high school sweetheart.

And what had once burned down to an ember now sparked as he watched her walk away.

* * *

Nicole spent the night in a luxurious suite at the Ritz, but she couldn't sleep a wink. It was bad enough that Miguel's refusal to help had left her in a real bind, but his rejection had opened old wounds she'd thought had healed long before.

Originally, she'd planned to extend her time in Manhattan long enough for her parents to think that she and Miguel had actually rekindled their romance. Instead, when she woke the next morning, she called the airline and paid to change her tickets, then took the next flight home—deflated.

Yet it was more than losing the company that had her unbalanced and dragging. It was seeing Miguel again, hoping he'd help her...

Then having him turn her down.

She could understand why he did, she supposed. After all, he couldn't very well leave a good job and come back to Red Rock at the drop of a hat.

Still, it was more than the old pain that her trip had stirred up, it was the old attraction, too. It had struck her when she'd first entered his office and found him standing beside his desk, with that dark hair a woman could run her fingers through and dark eyes that could make her whimper with a single glance.

The years had been good to him—and he was even more handsome than he'd been at seventeen, more appealing, more...tempting.

Last night, while seated across the candlelit table from him at dinner, he'd smiled at her, and the intensity in his gaze had sent her senses reeling. The teen-age Miguel had been a real charmer, and as a grown man, he'd clearly honed that skill to an art. It was hard to believe he wasn't married—or otherwise taken—and she wondered why that was.

In a lot of ways he'd changed, though. He might still have a playful side, but he seemed to be more serious now, more intense. He'd also abandoned his worn, frayed jeans and T-shirts for a trendy, fashionable style that suited his high-profile entertainment job.

She supposed that spending the past ten years in New York working in the music industry had made him different from the boy she once knew. Of course, it had also made him different from the other men she knew in Texas.

What had provoked her to think a guy like Miguel would come back to Red Rock, let alone go to the effort of pretending as though he still fit right in?

You've got to be kidding, Marnie had said when she'd heard of Nicole's plan to ask Miguel to marry her.

Too bad she hadn't been. It would have saved her the embarrassment of asking, then having him decline.

Now here she was, back in Red Rock and no closer to a solution than she'd been before.

After entering the five-story building that housed the offices of Castleton Boots, she took the elevator to the top floor, feeling defeated—yet not quite resigned.

What was she going to do now?

She had no idea, but she'd think of something—she had to.

"Good afternoon, Nicole." Diana Solares, the receptionist, offered her a smile as she entered the lobby. "I didn't expect you back so soon."

"The meeting was a quick one," she said.

"I hope it went well."

"As well as could be expected." And wasn't that the truth? Going to see Miguel, hoping that he still felt some sense of friendship or loyalty had been a pipe dream.

What had she been thinking?

Once she entered her personal office, with its wall-to-wall windows providing a view of downtown Red Rock, she took a seat at her cherrywood desk and began to look over the telephone messages Diana had left for her. She hadn't had a chance to return a single call when her father popped his head through the doorway and cleared his throat.

"You're back," he said. "That was quick."

"Yes, I'm back." After making eye contact, she looked down at the stack of messages, as if each one was so important it required an immediate response.

"I'd hoped you'd be able to spend some time in the city, maybe see a show or do some shopping."

So had she—but since Miguel had refused her offer, there hadn't been any need to remain in New York. She had work to do here—and a Plan B to come up with. In spite of the sleepless night she'd spent at the Ritz, she hadn't thought of any feasible options.

"You really ought to get out more," her father added. "You've been burning the candle at both ends ever since you graduated college and came back here to work. Just look at the circles under your eyes—"

"Dad! Drop it, please?"

"Drop what?"

"You and Mom are control freaks when it comes to me, and I'm getting tired of it. In case you've forgotten, I'm an adult."

"We haven't forgotten."

"Oh, no? Then let me decide when to vacation and when to sleep. And, for the record, I'll also decide who to marry—and when."

"I'm sorry, honey. I know what it must look like, but I really have your best interests at heart. And as much as I've loved the company, I've managed to keep a balance. My family always comes first. Without my wife and daughter, all my efforts at Castleton Boots wouldn't have been worth a dime. And your mom and I are afraid that, without our intervention, you might let your best years pass you by."

Nicole leaned back in her desk chair and crossed her arms. "I've poured my heart and soul into this company, Dad."

"That's the point. A company shouldn't be your heart and soul. Your family should. And while your mother and I are proud of your accomplishments, it's time for you to settle down. You're still young, and you deserve to have a life outside of the office."

"I'm happy with my life."

"Yes, but we're worried about the fact that you've

turned down suitor after suitor—and most of them were fine young men who would have made good husbands."

"Like who?" she asked.

"First off, there's Dr. Peter Wellington. You dated him three times, then quit taking his calls."

"Your golfing buddy? He's twenty years older than I am."

"He's also a surgeon."

"And he's about as interesting as the list of foods on a bland diet."

Her father chuffed. "You want younger? How about David Vandergrift? He's a Stanford grad."

"And he has absolutely no sense of humor."

"Gordon Boswell is funny."

"If you like guys who dress like rodeo clowns. Come on, Dad. Give me a break." Nicole shook her head. "You're so worried that I'll be an old maid, you went through a legal manipulation to force me to choose one of the men you and Mom keep pushing on me. All I want to do is take my rightful place at Castleton Boots, and you want to sell it to a stranger."

"It's not as though you wouldn't be the major stockholder. You'll never have any financial worries."

"It's not the money, Dad. It's being a part of all of this. And you're taking that away from me."

"You're not getting any younger, honey. And your mother had a very difficult time conceiving. Do I have to remind you that we were well into our forties when we had you?"

No, he didn't. Growing up, she'd had friends whose

grandparents had been younger than her parents. But that hadn't mattered to her. She loved her mother and father. And they'd adored her. There hadn't been anything they hadn't done for her, hadn't given her. That's what made rebelling against them so difficult.

Well, that and the fact that she could never win an argument with her dad. He always insisted upon having the last word.

"Your mom and I just don't want you to sacrifice your personal life for the company," he added. "And we don't want you to wake up one day with a bunch of regrets."

Nicole clicked her tongue. She had plenty of regrets already. But before she could respond, a deep and oh-so-familiar baritone voice sounded from the doorway. "Don't worry about Nicole's personal life. It's about to get a whole lot better."

Chapter Three

Nicole turned to the doorway, where Miguel stood with a colorful bouquet of flowers in his hands and a heart-stopping grin on his face. His expression was surely as phony as the story she'd hoped to concoct for her parents, but that didn't matter. He'd obviously had a change of heart, and for that she'd be eternally grateful.

But before she could welcome him in—and was he ever welcome!—he entered the office with a sexy Texas swagger and the assurance of a born-and-bred New Yorker.

"I'm sorry I'm late," he said, as he bent and brushed a kiss upon her cheek. "I stopped off to get you some flowers."

His musky scent sent her already-racing heart topsy-turvy, and as he turned to her father, she hoped her surprise wasn't plastered all over her face.

"Mr. Castleton," he said, extending his hand in greeting. "It's good to see you again, sir."

Nicole's dad looked at him blankly, as if he had no idea who he was or when they'd ever met. But then again, why would he remember? Her father had never bothered to give Miguel the time of day before.

Yet who would have guessed that the edgy, wisecracking teen would have morphed into a confident, clean-shaven executive wearing a designer suit?

"I'm sorry," her father said, as he reached out to shake Miguel's hand. "Have we met before?"

"A time or two, but it's been years. I'm Miguel Mendoza."

Even the mention of his name hadn't triggered her father's memory, because a furrowed brow indicated he was still trying to connect the dots.

"Please," her father said, "call me Andy."

"I'm sorry," Miguel said, as he turned to Nicole. "Didn't you tell him, honey?"

"Um…no, I didn't get a chance to do that yet." Nicole rolled back her desk chair and stood. "Daddy, Miguel and I reconnected a while ago—on Facebook. We've been in contact, and while I was in New York, we met up and…" She glanced at her old high school flame, looking for reinforcement and finding it in that dazzling smile.

"And one thing led to another," Miguel said, as he

finished her sentence and, at the same time, took a seat on the edge of her desk.

As the seventy-five-year-old CEO of Castleton Boots tried to wrap his mind around the significance of Miguel's arrival, his memory must have finally kicked in, because he stiffened. "What's this all about?"

"In spite of a ten-year separation, we realized that we still love each other." Miguel reached for Nicole's hand and gave it an affectionate squeeze. "I have dinner reservations for us at Red tonight, honey. I hope you're as hungry as I am."

She offered him a smile, yet was half-tempted to throttle him for not giving her a heads-up. It would have saved her a lot of grief to know that he was going to show up. And it would have been helpful to have a chance to get their stories straight.

Her father, clearly blindsided by the scene that had been created for his benefit, didn't speak, let alone object.

"Are you ready to go?" Miguel asked Nicole.

At that, her father rallied and found his voice. "It's only four o'clock, Nicole. And you just got here. Surely you aren't leaving now."

A breezy smile, the kind Nicole hadn't worn in years, slipped easily into place. "I'm trying to maintain a balance between work and my personal life, Daddy. Isn't that what you wanted?"

Again, her father fell silent—which wasn't his usual response to unexpected complications at work or at home. And Nicole realized her marriage scheme just might work out even better than she'd hoped.

Rather than give her father time to voice a rebuttal, Nicole slipped her arm through Miguel's, and they swept out of the office, leaving the stunned CEO behind.

When they reached the elevator and were safely out of earshot, she couldn't stop the bubble of laughter that burst out. "Did you see the look on his face?"

"He's at a loss, that's for sure." Miguel pushed the down button.

Once the doors opened, and they stepped inside, Nicole released her hold on Miguel's arm. "Actually, I'm at a loss, too. Don't get me wrong, I'm glad you're here. But what changed your mind?"

He shrugged. "The money, I suppose. I've lost a few dreams over the years, and with what you're offering me, I'll be able to achieve one of them."

The nightclub, she realized. And for some reason, the honesty of his answer—and the lack of anything emotional attached to it—didn't sit well.

So what was with that?

They rode down in silence. And when the elevator opened on the lobby floor, she asked, "Now what?"

"I was serious about dinner reservations. Why don't I pick you up at five-thirty? I know that's earlier than either of us are used to eating, but the sooner we get to Red, the sooner we can convince everyone in town that we're back together again."

So that was it for now? They'd left the office as a

couple who were in love, only to separate in the parking lot and go their own ways until later tonight?

Oh, for Pete's sake. What else did she expect?

"Five-thirty sounds good to me," she said.

"All I need is an address."

"Of course. I live in a condominium complex near Red Rock Country Club—Fairway Estates. I'm in number twenty-two. I'll leave your name at the gate."

"All right. I'll see you then." Miguel turned and headed for his vehicle, as if they'd merely had a business meeting that was now over.

But then again, isn't that what had just taken place?

Hadn't she offered him a hundred thousand dollars to sweeten the deal?

And it had worked, hadn't it?

So why had a dull ache settled in her chest as she watched him walk away and climb into a silver Ford Expedition?

There was no reason for it, no reason at all. So she shook it off and headed for her own car, a matador red Lexus sedan.

Who cared why he'd come back to Red Rock?

When push came to shove, she'd take Miguel Mendoza any way she could get him.

Miguel arrived at Nicole's condo at five-thirty on the dot. Hers was a corner unit, which provided a view of the lake on the seventh fairway. She invited him into her living room, which had been stylishly decorated in soft shades of brown, with splashes of red, yellow and green.

It must have cost a pretty penny, but then again, she and her family could certainly afford it.

Yet he found himself more interested in the way she'd pulled her hair into a chic twist, in the diamond studs that adorned her ears, in the perfect fit of the slinky black dress she wore.

"Can I get you something to drink?" she asked. "Lemonade, iced tea—maybe a glass of wine or a beer?"

"No, I think it's best if we get out of here and let the community see us as a couple."

"Good idea. But shouldn't we get our story straight first?"

"Let's just keep it simple. Like you said to your dad earlier—and great idea, by the way—we connected on Facebook a few months back, then met in person while you were in New York. The moment we laid eyes on each other, we fell in love all over again."

"Perfect," she said.

"Then shall we go?" he asked.

After she locked up her condo, she climbed into his rented SUV, and he drove her to Red, the family-owned restaurant that had once been a Spanish hacienda. Miguel's aunt and uncle, Jose and Maria Mendoza, owned the place and had gone out of their way to make sure they maintained a historical, as well as a cultural, ambiance.

"I've always loved this restaurant," Nicole said, "although I haven't been here in years."

He wondered if she'd avoided it so as not to run into

him or his family, just as he'd gone out of his way to avoid hers, but he didn't ask.

"I hear your aunt and uncle nearly lost this place in a fire," she added.

She was right. Four years ago, an arsonist had nearly destroyed the interior.

"It took several months for Jose and Maria to clean up the place and refurbish it," he said. "And a lot of the original furniture and furnishings were destroyed, but they managed to recreate a similar decor and were able to reopen."

As they entered Red, Nicole scanned the white-plaster walls, taking in the nineteenth century photographs, colorful southwestern blankets and artwork. "If I hadn't known about the fire, I probably wouldn't have noticed anything different."

Most of those who only occasionally patronized the restaurant wouldn't, either. But the Mendoza family, as well as the Red Rock Fortunes, were well aware of the various changes.

Lola Martinez, an old family friend who now worked part-time at the restaurant as a hostess, greeted Miguel with a hug. "*Mijo,* it's so good to see you. Marcos told me you'd be coming in tonight. So we reserved a table for you in the courtyard."

Marcos, Miguel's brother, managed the restaurant these days. And when he'd learned that Miguel was going to bring Nicole here, he'd promised to make sure their evening would be special.

If Marcos had been surprised by the news of the rekindled romance, he hadn't said anything. And Miguel was glad. He couldn't risk letting anyone know their relationship was fake.

It would be easier to pull off that way.

And this time, when Nicole ended things by filing for a divorce, Miguel wouldn't wear his heart on his sleeve, as he'd done when they'd split up as teenagers. Instead, he'd shake it off and focus on opening his first of several nightclubs, this one in downtown Red Rock. And when it caught on, like he knew it would, he'd open the next one in San Antonio. Because now that Miguel was back in Texas, he planned to stay and make the best of it.

"Come this way," Lola said, as she led Miguel and Nicole to the old-style courtyard with its Mexican tiled floor, rustic old fountain and lush green plants and bougainvillea that bloomed in bright shades of fuchsia, purple and gold.

As they took their seats at one of the pine tables shaded by a colorful umbrella, the sound of mariachi music coming from the lounge harmonized with the soft gurgle of the water in the fountain.

Nicole scanned the courtyard, then returned her bright-eyed gaze to Miguel. "I'd forgotten what a lovely atmosphere this restaurant has."

She was right, he supposed. But since he'd never brought a date here, he hadn't considered anything but the fact that the food was great and that it would be the perfect place for their first public appearance.

"Red is one of the most popular restaurants in town,

so we'll probably run into someone who knows us or our family and friends. It's a good way to get the word out that we're together again."

Nicole reached across the table and placed her hand over his, setting off an unexpected rush of heat. "Thanks again for coming back to Red Rock, Miguel. And for showing up at the office like you did. My dad seemed genuinely surprised to see you—and not the least bit skeptical of our engagement."

Miguel was glad their performance had been successful so far, but he also liked knowing that their news had unbalanced the man who'd crushed his teenage hopes and dreams.

But he wouldn't admit that to Nicole—or to anyone for that matter. It was best that she thought the money had been his motivation.

The busboy dropped off a basket of fresh tortilla chips at their table, as well as salsa *fresca* and two glasses of water with lemon slices, saying that Tom, their waiter, would be coming to take their drink orders.

Miguel planned to order a Corona with lime for himself, but just as the busboy turned away and the waiter approached, he had a second thought, a better one.

"Welcome to Red," the tall, gangly young man said. "My name is Tom. Shall I start you off with something to drink?"

"We'd like a bottle of your best champagne." Miguel glanced across the table at Nicole and flashed a grin her way. "We have a lot to celebrate, don't you think?"

She returned his smile. "Yes, we do."

Tom had no more gone in search of the champagne when Marcos stopped by their table and greeted them. Of all four Mendoza brothers, Marcos and Miguel were the most alike, especially in appearance. And as the youngest in the family, just two years apart, they'd become friends as well as brothers.

Now twenty-nine, Marcos managed Red and was doing a great job of it. But like Miguel, he had higher aspirations than to spend his life working for someone else. He dreamed of opening his own restaurant one day soon.

The brothers greeted each other, but only briefly since they'd met earlier this afternoon.

"Nicole," Marcos said, reaching out his hand to shake hers. "It's good to see you again. It's been a long time."

"Too long," Miguel said. "But we're about to remedy that."

Marcos lobbed her an easy grin. "Miguel told me the good news earlier today. Congratulations. I hope you'll be as happy as Wendy and I are."

A year ago last December, Marcos married one of the Atlanta Fortunes. He and Wendy had a daughter they both adored. And who wouldn't? MaryAnne was a beautiful child, a toddler who was their pride and joy.

Was it any wonder Marcos would want the same happiness for his younger brother?

Yet Miguel's marriage would be a sham, a fact that released a shimmy of guilt in his gut.

"I'll admit," Marcos added, "the whole thing seemed

a little sudden. But I knew how much you guys cared for each other in high school."

And Marcos, more than anyone, had known just how hard Miguel had taken the breakup.

But, hey. So what? Teenagers didn't realize that life went on, that the world didn't revolve around a single girl.

"I'm glad you found each other again," Marcos added. "You have a lot of catching up to do."

"Actually," Miguel said, "we're going to cut to the chase. We've wasted enough time already, so we plan to get married right away."

At that, Nicole, who'd just taken a sip of water, choked and sputtered. "Excuse me."

Surely she hadn't been surprised by his comment. Or disappointed to think she wouldn't get to participate in all that bridal stuff.

"So when's the big day?" Marcos asked.

Nicole cleared her throat. "We don't have a date set, although it'll be in the near future."

Miguel shot a glance across the table, saw her biting down on her bottom lip.

What was that all about? For a woman who'd been so determined to create a marriage that she'd flown all the way to New York to make an old boyfriend an offer he couldn't refuse, she seemed to be dragging her feet now. And he couldn't help wondering why.

Was she afraid to follow through with this challenge to her parents?

"We want to get married as soon as possible," Nicole explained, "but I'd rather not elope. Besides, there's also a seventy-two-hour waiting period for a marriage license. So we'll have to wait at least a week anyway."

"That still sounds like a whirlwind courtship to me," Marcos said.

And it was. But unless Miguel had misunderstood Nicole, that had been her game plan. Hadn't it?

Tom the waiter approached with an ice bucket and a tray bearing two champagne flutes and a bottle of Cristal. "Will this be okay?"

"Perfect." Miguel watched as his brother scanned the room, caught the eye of one of his employees, then nodded.

"You'll have to excuse me," Marcos said, "I have to go now, but I'll stop by again before you leave. You can tell me more about your wedding plans then."

As Marcos walked away, the waiter popped the cork, then poured them each a glass. When they were finally alone again, Miguel raised his flute for a toast, and Nicole followed his lead.

"To young love," he said. "And to a successful business venture."

He supposed he could have come up with something a lot more romantic, but for now, they were the only two in the courtyard, and addressing the real reason for their reunion seemed to be a lot more fitting.

As their glasses clinked, and the crystal resonated in the air, footsteps sounded on the tile floor.

Miguel looked up to see the approaching diners, only

to recognize his half sister, Isabella, and her husband, J.R. Fortune.

Isabella, with her long dark hair and big brown eyes, was a lovely woman who always chose bright colorful apparel that reflected her Tejano heritage, like the southwestern print skirt and matching red blouse she wore tonight. When she scanned the courtyard and spotted her youngest brother, her eyes lit up. "Miguel! I didn't know you were in town. Why didn't you call?"

Miguel got to his feet, greeted Isabella with a hug, then shook J.R.'s hand. "I'd planned to surprise you guys." He glanced down at Nicole. "I'm not sure if you remember Nicole Castleton, Isabella."

Momentarily stunned to silence, his lovely and gracious sister quickly recovered. "Of course I do. It's been a long time."

"Yes," Nicole said. "It has."

Miguel knew his sister would be pumping him for details later. And apparently, J.R. had some questions, too, because the Los Angeles businessman turned Red Rock rancher said, "You'll have to come out to Molly's Pride for dinner one night while you're in town."

J.R. had named his ranch after his late mother, Molly. And he and Isabella had done an amazing job refurbishing the old hacienda and making it into a home.

"Yes," Isabella said. "You'll have to see what we've done to the courtyard and the patio. We've added a new built-in barbecue and a garden."

J.R. added, "I hope you'll be around longer than last time you were in town, Miguel."

For the past ten years, Miguel had only come home for Christmas or an occasional Thanksgiving, staying only a day or two. Of course, he'd spent more time in town when Javier had been in the hospital last spring.

"Actually," he said, "I'll be in Red Rock indefinitely. And dinner sounds great. I hope you don't mind if I bring Nicole with me."

Isabella brightened. "Not at all. In fact, I'd be disappointed if you didn't."

Ever since Isabella had returned to Red Rock in search of her father and his family, her four half brothers had accepted her unconditionally. She'd come back about the time Miguel and Nicole had split up, so she'd been aware of Miguel's heartbreak and his decision to leave Red Rock.

She also knew that he'd suffered two big losses in his life—first Nicole, then, more recently, his mother who'd died of pneumonia. So her happiness was sincere.

Again, he tamped down the guilt that rose up inside. Did he really have to deceive his family, especially Isabella?

Should he level with her later, when Nicole wasn't around?

"But what do you mean by 'indefinitely'?" Isabella asked. "Aren't you still working for Home Run Records?"

"I took a leave of absence," Miguel said.

"Why?"

"Because Nicole and I are getting married."

"Married?" Isabella turned briefly to J.R., who had

to be about as surprised as she was, then back to Miguel. "That's wonderful. Have you set a date?"

"Actually," Miguel said, "I haven't officially proposed yet, so we haven't made any kind of formal announcement or settled on dates. I'd like to do it as soon as possible, but Nicole wants to wait."

At that point, Nicole thought she'd better step in and explain. "It's not that I'm dragging my feet. There's just so much to do. I'm going to need at least two weeks to get it all done."

Isabella offered her an understanding smile. "You're right about all that needs to be done. And two weeks is still considered a whirlwind courtship."

Nicole shot up a glance at Miguel, trying to read his expression. She was glad that he was embracing his role so enthusiastically, but his sudden turnaround made her a little uneasy, although she wasn't sure why.

"I'd love to help any way I can," Isabella said. "Why don't you come to the ranch for lunch on Saturday afternoon? We can talk about it then."

"That's really nice of you," Nicole said, "but—"

Miguel reached down and placed his hand over hers, branding her with the warmth of his touch. "Let her do it, honey."

The warmth in his eyes seemed so real that she had to remind herself it was all an act, that they weren't really in love, that their engagement was as phony as a three-dollar bill.

"I'm so happy for you, guys," Isabella said.

"So am I." The tall, fair-haired rancher slipped his

arm around his wife's shoulder and drew her close. "If you'd like to have the ceremony on Molly's Pride, you're more than welcome to do so. All you have to do is say the word."

"Thank you," Miguel said. "We might take you up on that."

Yes, Nicole thought. They might. Her parents, of course, had always imagined her wedding would be a big formal affair. But she doubted they'd be on board for this one. They were sure to object—about the venue, the size…the groom.

"We'd like to keep things small and intimate," Nicole said.

"Whatever you want is fine with me," Isabella said. "And I'd love to help with the planning. I'll get your number from Miguel and give you a call tomorrow. We'll set a time for lunch, and we can talk about a guest list for the wedding."

The wedding.

A guest list.

Family and friends.

Gifts.

Yikes!

She'd better not open anything, especially if she had to give it all back. The game plan that had sounded so promising just moments ago now threatened to blow sky-high if she wasn't careful.

"Miguel and I are still talking over the details," she told his sister.

"Good. I'll call you tomorrow and you can let me

know what you've decided. I love weddings. It'll be fun having yours on the ranch—unless you prefer having it elsewhere."

Right now, Las Vegas was sounding pretty good.

"Well," J.R. said, "we'd better let you get back to your celebration. Congratulations. This is a very nice surprise."

"It certainly is." Isabella offered Nicole another warm, sincere smile.

And with that, they continued on their way through the courtyard and to the front of the restaurant.

"What's the matter?" Miguel asked. "You look as if you're having second thoughts."

"Oh, no. It's not that. It's just that… Well, it's the whole gift idea. Deceiving my parents is one thing. After all, they set this whole thing in motion when they placed such unreasonable demands on me. But I don't like lying to your family." She glanced at Isabella and J.R., watching their backs until they disappeared from sight. Under the circumstances, she'd expected them to be… Well, skeptical to say the least, especially after their teenage romance ended in heartbreak.

Why had they been so supportive, so welcoming?

"I don't like lying to my family, either," Miguel said. "I wish I could confide in them, but the more people who know what's really going on, the more chance that your parents will learn what you're doing."

Nicole bit back her momentary apprehension. What other option did she have?

The waiter had no more than taken their dinner orders when her cell phone rang. Normally, she would have ignored the interruption and focused on her dinner companion, especially one who was so handsome and intriguing, but an overactive work ethic insisted she at least check the display to see who was trying to reach her.

When she recognized her mother's number, she looked across the table at Miguel. "It's my mom."

"News certainly travels fast. Go ahead and take it."

She waited a beat, then answered. "Hello?"

"Nicole, it's Mom. Your father tells me that you've been seeing that boy again."

Nicole rolled her eyes. It was as if she'd never left high school! "That boy is twenty-eight years old and an executive of a record company. He's also the love of my life—and the man I intend to marry." She shot a glance across the table, caught Miguel's gaze. For a moment, a connection formed between them. Yet not the kind she could tie her heart to. Not anymore.

"I realize that you once had feelings for him," her mother began.

"I still do, and they've only grown stronger, Mom. It's amazing, but after ten years, I realize why no other men have ever appealed to me." The words had no more than rolled out of her mouth when she realized there might be a wee bit of truth to them.

As the daughter of one of the richest men in Red Rock, she'd always been in high demand as a date. But for all the proper young men introduced to her—first at the debutante balls then later, when she'd reached adulthood, at charity benefits, dinner parties and other so-cial events—no one she'd ever met had made her heart race. Not the way Miguel had when they were teens.

"Your father and I hope you won't do anything hasty and that you'll take time to get to know that young man. After all, he's been away for so long. He's not the same person anymore. And neither are you."

At that, Nicole couldn't help but chuckle at the ab-surdity of it all. "Now wait a minute, I thought you two worried that life was passing me by, that I was too fo-cused on work."

"Yes, but that doesn't mean we want you to marry the first guy who—"

"The first guy who what? Came along and caught my eye ten years ago? Seriously, Mom. I never should have let you and Daddy talk me into breaking up with Miguel in the first place. Who knows what our lives might have been like if we'd had a chance to let our feel-ings grow and develop. We might have gotten married years ago—and had a couple children by now. And as far as we're concerned…" She glanced across the table, saw Miguel watching her intently, as if she were mak-ing a long overdue confession. And in a way, maybe she was. "Well, as far as we're concerned, we're not going to waste any more time. We plan to marry within the next two weeks—if not sooner. And you and Daddy can choose to be supportive and attend the small cer-emony—or not."

There. She'd said it. The marriage was on—deception and all.

Her mother waited for what seemed like forever before saying, "You can't blame us for worrying. We love you, honey. And we do want to be supportive. Why don't you just slow down a bit and let Daddy and I catch our breaths."

"I don't plan to wait long," Nicole said.

Her mother paused for a moment, catching her breath, it seemed. "Maybe we should talk more about this over dinner tomorrow night."

"Only if I can bring Miguel."

Another pause, this one lasting two beats. "All right. I'll reserve one of the private rooms at the country club."

Nicole glanced across the table. "I'll have to ask Miguel if he's available for dinner tomorrow."

When he nodded, she told her mother okay.

"Then we'll see you at six," her mom said.

When the call ended, Nicole placed her cell back in her purse. "Well, we certainly have their attention."

Before Miguel could respond, Tom returned with their dinner—beef fajitas for him and a chicken tostada for her. And while the food was tasty, Nicole merely picked at hers.

"What's the matter?" he asked.

"Nothing."

"Are you sorry you set all this into motion?"

"No, not at all." She had no problem with the marriage plan itself.

But how many people would get caught up in the deception?

She scanned the courtyard, noting that it had filled with other diners.

As Miguel's chair scraped against the tile floor, she turned to the sound and watched him stand. As he stepped away from the table, she assumed he was going to excuse himself to go to the men's room. Instead, he cleared his throat. Then, in a booming voice, he said, "Nicole Castleton, I have a confession to make."

What was going on?

She had no idea. And obviously, the other diners were just as curious because their voices grew quiet, their heads turned and their movements stilled.

As Miguel dropped to one knee beside her, he reached into the lapel of his jacket, pulled out a small velvet box and flipped open the lid, revealing a modestly sized but sparkling diamond ring.

"I let you get away from me once because I was young and afraid to fight for what I wanted. But I won't make that mistake again."

He let *her* get away?

"Will you marry me, Nicole? Will you be my wife, the mother of my children? Will you be my best friend, my lover, my partner for the rest of my life?"

Tears welled in her eyes, and emotion clogged her throat. At one time, she'd dreamed of a night like this one, hoped for a proposal like this. Yet as surreal, romantic and magical as this evening was, it had been bought and paid for. And that bittersweet reality made for a bride who was blushing and teary-eyed for all the wrong reasons.

She should have followed her cue by blurting out a happy yes—and she would, if she could. Instead, she merely nodded.

As if Miguel understood all that swirled around inside her heart, he smiled and got to his feet. Then he reached for her hand, drew her to stand alongside him and slipped the glistening diamond onto her finger.

As the other diners, including J.R. and Isabella, clapped and cheered, Miguel wrapped his arms around her and drew her into his embrace.

Thank goodness one of them had some kind of an internal script to follow, even an imaginary one, because she was at a complete loss on where to go from here.

That is, until he lowered his lips to hers.

Chapter Four

Once the kiss began, there was no need to follow any script or game plan. All the stumbling blocks slipped away, and everything fell into place.

In spite of the audience they now had and all the changes that had taken place in the last ten years, they seemed to take up right where they'd last left off.

Nicole's lips parted without conscious thought, and Miguel's tongue slipped into her mouth. The arousing, woodsy scent of his cologne, combined with the taste of him, sparked a hunger she hadn't known in ages. And the kiss deepened until she thought her knees might buckle if she didn't hold on for dear life.

When they finally came up for air, another cheer went out in the crowded courtyard, followed by applause. She supposed she ought to be a bit embarrassed by the very public display of affection—well, make that *feigned* affection. Yet in spite of the staged performance, their passion seemed to burn as hot as it ever had.

She reached for Miguel's forearm to steady herself, afraid she might sway on her feet if she didn't.

How could the man do that to her with a single kiss? And after all these years?

"Come on," he said. "Let's go home."

Home. The word had such a nice sound to it, especially when Miguel was the one saying it. And she couldn't help thinking about the two of them returning to her condo after a dinner date. It made them seem like a real couple, fully committed and facing the future together.

In a way, she supposed they *were* committed now, at least to her business proposition and to the temporary marriage he'd agreed to. But their futures were heading in different directions once they filed for a divorce.

As they left the courtyard and headed toward the front of the restaurant, Nicole continued to hold Miguel's arm with her left hand, where the diamond she now wore sparkled on her ring finger.

She wondered where he'd found it. Had he borrowed it from a friend? Was it on loan from a jeweler?

Had he actually purchased it? If he had, she'd have to reimburse him for the expense.

As they crossed the parking lot to his car, he said, "By morning, everyone in Red Rock will know—and better yet, believe—that we're engaged."

After that mind-numbing kiss, which had been all she'd remembered and more, Nicole could almost believe they were really engaged, too.

He opened the car door for her, and she slid into the passenger seat. Moments later, they were on their way back to her condo. They didn't talk much on the drive home. She supposed that was because there was so much to think about, at least on her part. But what about him?

Was he pondering the financial offer she'd made him and his plans to finally open the nightclub he'd dreamed about?

Maybe he was more focused on the phony engagement they'd set into motion tonight and the lie they'd be living until she finally became CEO of Castleton Boots and held the controlling share of stock.

Or was he, like her, amazed by the kiss they'd just shared and the passion that still sizzled between them?

To be honest, she was a bit concerned by the chemistry that hadn't waned, especially since she had a business arrangement with him she didn't want to complicate. It was imperative that she keep her head about her until they were married and she'd fulfilled the legal stipulations her parents had set up. Then they could file for divorce and go their own way.

When they reached the guard at the gate, Nicole identified herself as a resident, and he let them into the Spanish-style complex. Then Miguel drove to the curb in front of her home, a two-story unit with a white stucco exterior, dark wood trim and a red tile roof.

"Thank you for dinner," she said. "And for giving such a great performance at Red."

"My pleasure."

Should she invite him inside? Probably so, but then what? Her heart rate skipped into overdrive at the thought—and at all the invitation could lead to.

Miguel opened the driver's door and got out of the car. She wasn't sure if he planned to open her door for her or not, but she decided to make it easy on both of them by exiting the vehicle on her own.

The light fragrance of night-blooming jasmine filled the evening air as they made their way to the entrance of her condo, the soles of their shoes clicking on the sidewalk.

Again, she thought about inviting him in for a cup of coffee or a nightcap, weighing the options.

When they reached her front door, which was flanked by terra-cotta pots bearing lush red hibiscus, he said, "I'll bring over my suitcase and shaving kit tomorrow. I think it's best if I move in. Don't you?"

She supposed he had a point.

"People would probably expect that," she said. "Under the circumstances."

Yet how far should she and Miguel go in proving they were a real couple, that they were truly in love and planning to marry?

Right now, as they stood on her porch, with a blanket of twinkling stars and a lovers' moon glowing overhead, his gaze zeroed in on her, she couldn't help thinking they should go all the way.

But she shook off the rogue thought. Before she could open her mouth to end their evening together, he said, "Can you get me a resident's pass for the gate? I'll also need a spare key to your place. Unless you have an objection, I'll stop by your office tomorrow and pick it up there."

"I..." She swallowed, trying to find the words, trying to put her thoughts together. "I have a spare I can give you now."

"I think it might work better if I get it tomorrow. That way, even if the Red Rock rumor mill hasn't gotten the word out, everyone in the office will know that I'm the new man in your life—and that I'm here to stay."

Here to stay. That had a nice ring to it, too. But in truth, his stay was only temporary. And not just because their marriage wasn't going to last. She'd recently purchased a new house on the edge of town and planned to move at the end of the month. But there was no need to explain that now.

"You seem to have thought of everything." She lifted her left hand. "A ring, a public proposal..."

That amazing, courtyard-spinning kiss also came to mind, but she didn't dare mention that.

"Yeah, well the people I work with refer to me as the idea man—and for good reason." A grin tugged at one side of his mouth, giving her a glimpse of the cocky but charming teenage boy he'd once been. "Anyway, I'd better go. I'll see you tomorrow."

He was leaving?

Without coming inside?

And without a good-night kiss?

She fought the compulsion to reach for his hand, to ask him to wait, to invite him in.

But things were moving so fast.

Too fast, maybe. So she said, "Good night, Miguel. And thanks again."

"My pleasure," he said for the second time tonight, tossing her a smile as if he really meant it. Then he turned and walked back to the SUV.

As she watched him open the driver's door and slide behind the wheel, a wave of disappointment swept through her.

And she'd be darned if she knew why.

Miguel arrived at Nicole's office the next morning at ten. Last night, he'd told her that he wanted to make a show of getting the spare key in front of her coworkers, and while that had been a good idea, it had only been an excuse to leave before she invited him inside. And she would have done it; he was sure of it.

But why wouldn't she? That blasted kiss they'd shared following his proposal had left him struggling to breathe. And he knew it had thrown her for a loop, too.

Still, he hadn't been prepared to talk about it—if she'd been inclined to do so.

Strangely enough, he'd never cut bait and run in a situation like that before, never had to. In fact, if she'd been any other woman, he wouldn't have let an opportunity like that slip by him. He would have taken advantage of their obvious physical attraction and chemistry by kissing her deeply in the moonlight until she'd not only invited him into the house, but into her bed.

Of course, he'd had a few regrets on the walk back to the car, but he hadn't wanted to complicate things until he'd had a chance to think through all the ramifications.

And he'd had plenty of time to do that while in bed last night, since he'd lain awake considering the pros and cons of instigating a sexual relationship between them, no matter how brief or temporary their marriage or engagement might be.

So now, as he made his way to her private office, he planned to play the love-struck fiancé to the hilt.

Nicole wanted him to marry her. And she wanted their relationship to look believable to her parents, as well as to everyone in Red Rock.

The way he saw it, that meant they ought to be sleeping together.

In fact, the more he thought about making love with her, the more he liked the idea. Even when they were young, inexperienced and confined to the backseat of a car, sex had been amazing. So he didn't think she'd object.

And if she did?

He doubted it would take much to convince her to see things his way. Besides, he'd never had a problem charming a woman before, and he was going to charm the socks—and a lot more than that—off his future "bride."

As he strode down the hall, he saw that the door to her office was open. He paused in the doorway, watching her work. Her long, dark hair was pulled back in an elegant twist as she studied several spreadsheets on her desk.

She wore a gray business suit today—and another pair of killer heels. And while she looked the part of a stylish executive, she still nibbled her bottom lip the way she used to back in study hall.

Finally, he couldn't keep quiet any longer. "You know what they say about all work and no play."

When she turned and looked across the room, her lips, which bore only a trace of the lipstick she'd applied earlier, parted.

"How long have you been standing there?"

"Long enough to think you're due for a break."

A slow smile slid across her lips. "Thanks, but there's a board of directors meeting I need to attend, and it starts in about fifteen minutes. So I'm afraid that break will have to wait."

"Did you bring the spare house key?"

She nodded, then reached into a drawer and pulled out her purse—a fairly new Louis Vuitton. "I've fixed up the guest room for you—and stocked the bathroom with clean towels and toiletries. If there's anything else you need, let me know. I'll pick it up on my way home."

The guest room, huh? Well, he'd have to remedy that.

As Miguel crossed the room to get the key, a woman peered into the doorway. "Nicole? Rodney set up that PowerPoint presentation for you in the boardroom."

"Thanks, Diana."

Miguel cleared his throat, letting both women know

he was still in the room. "I don't want to bother you, honey. I just came to get your key. I'll be all moved in by the time you get home. And I'll have a bottle of champagne chilled and ready."

Diana straightened, and her eyes darted from Nicole to Miguel and back again, but she didn't say a word.

"Don't forget," Nicole said. "We're meeting my mother and father for dinner at the club tonight."

While the last thing in the world Miguel wanted to do was dress up and go to "the club" to meet her parents and deal with their snooty attitudes, that's what Nicole was paying him to do. So he would put on the granddaddy of all shows for them—even if the whole thing chapped his hide.

But he managed a happy-go-lucky smile for Diana's sake. "I won't forget. We have a lot to celebrate."

Poor Diana had to be reeling from the news and drowning in curiosity, especially if Nicole had all but given up her personal life for the company, so Miguel filled in a few of the blanks by tossing out a question to Nicole.

"Did you request that vacation time for our honeymoon yet?"

The question seemed to stun Nicole for a moment, but she rallied. "I planned to do it at lunchtime." Then she turned to Diana. "I'm sorry for being rude. This wonderful man is Miguel Mendoza, my fiancé. We haven't set an actual wedding date yet, but it'll be within the next couple of weeks."

"It's nice to meet you," Diana said to Miguel. And

then, turning back to Nicole, she added, "What a surprise. You spend so much time at the office, I didn't realize you'd met someone special."

"We knew each other years ago, met up again in New York and…" Nicole glanced at Miguel and smiled, her eyes lighting up as if they'd actually created a few romantic memories in Manhattan. "Well, one thing led to another, and…" She lifted her left hand and flashed the diamond, which seemed a lot bigger in the jewelry store—and not so impressive on her slender finger and next to that expensive Louis Vuitton purse.

"Congratulations," Diana said.

With her right hand, Nicole gave the key to Miguel. "Here you go. I'll be home by five-thirty. Dinner reservations are at six."

"I'll be ready." Miguel brushed a kiss on Nicole's lips. "Knock 'em dead at that meeting, babe." After flashing his most charming smile at Diana, he slipped the key to Nicole's condo into his pocket, then sauntered down the hall, out the door and to the elevator.

He wasn't sure how long their business arrangement would last, but he planned to make the most of his time in Red Rock.

And the most of his nights living with Nicole.

Nicole's parents still lived in the house where she grew up, a sprawling estate that overlooked the exclusive Red Rock Country Club, not far from her condominium. And while Miguel didn't mind having dinner with them this evening, he'd been a little put off by their invitation to meet them at the club, rather than at their home.

He couldn't help wondering if that was their way of maintaining formality and distance. After all, they hadn't made any real secret of the fact that they hadn't liked him before. With their haughty silence, they'd let him know that, in their opinion, he hadn't been good enough for Princess Nicole. And he had every reason to believe they wouldn't feel any differently now.

He wasn't about to let that bother him, though. He'd dealt with some hardened executives and entertainment moguls over the years, and he'd always held his own. He'd even put a few of them in their places, when he had to.

Earlier this afternoon, he'd moved into Nicole's guest room. But he didn't intend for that sleeping arrangement to last very long. Still, he settled in and waited for her to get home.

Just as she'd said, she arrived at five-thirty.

"You look great," she said, when she spotted him in a jacket and tie.

"I assumed there was a dress code."

"You're right. I forgot to mention it."

Yeah, well, in spite of what her parents might think, he wasn't a country bumpkin. He knew how to dress in formal settings.

"Give me just a minute," Nicole said, as she slipped out of her pumps and headed for her bedroom. "I need to freshen up, but it won't take long."

Five minutes later, she came out wearing a flowing

red dress and strappy sandals. She'd reapplied her lipstick and let her long brown hair fall softly along her
shoulders. She was a beautiful woman, the kind a man
liked having on his arm.

"I'm ready," she said.

On the outside, maybe. But he suspected she wasn't
so carefully put together on the inside. He didn't mention it, though.

Instead, he opened the door for her, and five minutes
later, they'd made the short drive to the country club.

After parking the car, they entered the main club-
house. Nicole stopped to speak to the receptionist, a
redhead in her mid-to-late thirties.

"We're here to meet my parents for dinner," Nicole
told her.

The receptionist offered them a friendly smile.
"They're in the Sportsman Room, waiting for you. It's
down the hall, the third door on the right."

As Nicole turned to follow the woman's directions,
Miguel took her by the hand and pulled her back. "Not
so fast, darlin'."

She stopped, turned and gave his fingers a little
squeeze. "I'm sorry, Miguel. I keep forgetting that I'm
not in this alone."

"You're more nervous than you should be."

She shook her head. "No, not really. It's all going to
happen, whether they like it or not. It's just that I always have to brace myself for the challenge, for the ar-
guments. And to be honest, I'd prefer to be home with

you this evening, having a glass of that chilled champagne you mentioned to Diana."

Miguel grinned. "For the record, so would I. But I've got your back, honey. And if things get out of hand, leave it all up to me."

She cocked her pretty head to the side, yet her hand still held his.

"I'm the idea man, remember?"

With that, she smiled, and her eyes lit up. "So you said. What do you have up your sleeve this time?"

"I'm going to give you a little shot of courage before you enter that dining room."

Her brow furrowed, and he could see the wheels turning. Did she think he'd brought a sterling silver flask of ninety proof with him?

"Trust me," he said. "Lead the way."

They walked several paces down the hall.

"It's just up ahead," Nicole said.

"Hold up a minute." Miguel slowed to a stop.

She did, too, and turned to face him again, confusion clouding her expression.

"Now for that infusion of courage." As he caught her gaze, he released her hand. Then he cupped her face, his thumbs caressing her cheeks in slow, sensuous strokes. "I think you're going to need an extra-strong dose of it tonight."

Then he lowered his mouth to hers with a tenderness that nearly surprised him.

Just as she'd done the last time they'd kissed, she leaned into him and wrapped her arms around him. As her lips parted, he sought her tongue with his, finding, tasting, mating.

A door clicked opened, but Miguel continued to hold her close, to kiss her deeply, to savor her taste, her floral scent.

When a throat cleared loud and forcibly, Miguel finally drew his mouth from hers.

"Is that really necessary?" Andy Castleton asked from the doorway to the private dining room.

Miguel and Nicole looked at each other and grinned, yet neither spoke.

"Well, don't just stand there," the silver-haired businessman said. "Get in here before you make a spectacle of yourselves."

Miguel didn't like taking orders, particularly from a man who expected everyone to hop to it whenever he spoke, so he lingered a moment longer than necessary.

As Andy clucked his tongue and returned to the table, where his wife waited, Miguel took Nicole by the hand again and gave it a squeeze. "How are you feeling *now?*"

Nicole laughed. "Like I can leap tall buildings in a single bound."

Ten minutes later, after a few stiff formalities, Miguel and Nicole sat across from Andy and Elizabeth Castleton, sipping an expensive bottle of Napa Valley merlot.

The white linen-draped table had been set with china, crystal and silver and adorned with a crystal vase filled with yellow roses.

"Nicole says you plan to open a nightclub," Elizabeth Castleton said.

"Yes, I do." He'd had the plans drawn up, even though he hadn't found a building to lease or to buy. But seeing the blueprints meant his dream was finally taking shape. And after Nicole paid him for marrying her and helping her out of a legal jam, he'd be able to take the next steps.

And it felt damn good to know he'd see the grand opening of Mendoza's in the near future.

"You know," Andy said, "I commend you for trying to do something for yourself, but managing a nightclub will keep you up late at night and at work on weekends. I can see where that will create problems on the home front. What kind of life is that for a man who expects to have a happy wife and family?"

Miguel tensed. His first thought was to tell Nicole's father to take a flying leap—or something not nearly as polite and with words that were inappropriate for mixed company. The arrogant bastard had shot down his hopes and dreams once before, and he wouldn't stand idly by and let it happen again.

But before he could answer, Nicole jumped in. "Don't worry about the time Miguel will need to spend away from home. We'll work through that."

Andy frowned and reached for his wineglass.

A shroud of silence stretched across the room until Elizabeth addressed her daughter. "How's the new house coming along, honey? I'm not sure why you insisted upon moving away from the country club—and outside the city limits. You're in a better place now. You could have purchased that lot just down the street from us if you wanted more room."

"I didn't want more property, Mom."

Miguel hadn't realized Nicole was planning a move. He wished she would have mentioned it. That's the kind of thing a woman's fiancé ought to know about.

"Your condo was professionally decorated. And it's so close. Besides, this community is safe and secure. If you ever have to go home alone late at night—"

"I'll have Miguel to come home to from now on," Nicole said. "He just moved in with me."

The Castletons both straightened, clearly taken aback by her announcement.

Miguel hadn't expected anything different from them, yet their reactions still stung.

"Nicole," her father said, "you know how your mother and I feel about that sort of thing. You two shouldn't live together until after the wedding, assuming you actually go through with it."

Assuming they went through with it?

For a guy who'd always kept his emotions and reactions in check, Miguel felt compelled to climb over the table and grab the older man by his dapper, two-hundred-dollar silk tie. But he fought the impulse, donned a rakish grin and said, "Oh, there'll be a wedding. And like it or not, we'll have a honeymoon, too."

One that would start tonight, if he had his way.

Miguel glanced across the table, caught Andy's gaze and held it in a silent challenge. Prior to this evening, he'd wanted to make love with Nicole for all the right reasons. But as her father drew an invisible line in the sand, there was a wrong reason, too.

He was going to enjoy getting back at the Castletons.

Chapter Five

If Miguel had felt the least bit uncomfortable eating dinner with Andy and Elizabeth Castleton at the Red Rock Country Club last night, he certainly hadn't shown it.

There'd been a moment when Nicole had suspected that he'd let down his guard, that he'd taken offense at her father's obvious displeasure at their renewed romance. But it had passed as quickly as she'd sensed it flare.

"So what's the deal with the new house?" Miguel asked, as they drove back to her condo.

"There's a new development outside the Red Rock city limits that I spotted a while back, and it really appealed to me. A few weeks ago, I purchased one of the houses. Escrow will close soon, and I'll be moving."

"It's too bad your parents aren't more supportive."

"I know. You'd think that I planned to move across the country. But to be honest, I don't care. Part of the appeal of that particular development was the fact that it's a twenty-minute drive from their house."

"Too bad you can't put more distance between you than that," he said.

"For the most part, they mean well."

He chuffed. "Rather than standing up to them, you decided it would be easier to sell your house and buy another."

"I just stood up to them *now*. I'm marrying a man they don't really know or approve of, and I've let him move in with me."

Okay, so she'd also hired him, rather than resign as VP of Castleton Boots to make her point, a stand she hadn't been ready to take. Because while her father loved her unconditionally, she knew he could play hardball when it came to the company. And she wasn't sure if she'd win the challenge or not.

"But you're right," she admitted. "I haven't always stood my ground with them, and it's high time I did. That sneaky legal maneuver they tried to pull really opened my eyes."

He didn't respond, so she added, "For what it's worth, I didn't just buy the house on a whim or because of its location. It has a cottage style that appeals to me in a lot of ways. And believe it or not, I've never been the country club type."

"You could have fooled me."

She stole another glance at him, trying to read his expression. What had he meant by that? She didn't play golf or tennis.

But she let it drop. Instead, she addressed his big move to New York. Did he think he was somehow more independent because of it?

"So why did you leave Red Rock? Were you trying to distance yourself from your family?"

"No, I just needed to get out on my own. I love my family, and we're still very close. They might not have liked the idea of me moving out of state, but they respected me and my choices enough to not stand in my way."

"Are you saying that's not the case with my family?"

He turned in his seat, his gaze reaching across the console and locking onto hers with an intensity that might make a weaker woman lean back. "I don't like that way your father patronizes me, but I can take it. What really burns me is the way he treats you."

"He loves me."

"I'm not doubting that. But he doesn't respect you, Nic. And you've earned that respect time and time again."

She wanted to argue, yet she appreciated his support, his confidence in her. And she had to admit there was some truth to what he said.

Miguel pulled in front of her condo and parked at the curb, but rather than shut off the ignition, he turned in his seat and faced her. "Look at you. You're not only bright, but beautiful. You're also outgoing, kind and generous. In high school you got along with the jocks and cheerleaders, as well as the math geeks. And I'm sure that's still true when it comes to business. You could hold the world in your hands—given the chance."

"Thanks, Miguel. I appreciate that. But people always seem to make assumptions about me based on my appearance—or my last name."

"That's hard not to do. It's one reason you had so many guys wanting to date you in high school."

Maybe so, but only one of them had ever gotten to first base—Miguel Mendoza, the teenage heartthrob who'd grown into the handsome man sitting across from her now.

"So tell me," he said. "How many other guys were in the running when you had to find a husband?"

To be honest? Not a single one. But that wasn't because she'd never gone out with anyone since Miguel. In fact, after college, she'd dated extensively for a while. But in the past couple of years, she hadn't found the time. So it was no wonder that she'd yet to meet "the one."

"It's been a while since I've been in a serious relationship," she admitted.

"That surprises me. I would have thought you would have been married already. I hope you aren't buying into your parents' hype that no one is good enough for their little princess."

"Of course not."

In college, and then again a couple of years back, she'd actively dated, searching for Mr. Right. But she hadn't met anyone who'd interested her enough to invest in a long-term relationship. And then, more recently, as she began to ascend the corporate ladder, she'd become too focused on work to take time for romance.

She'd considered another possibility, though. Marnie had once suggested that she held each of her potential boyfriends up to the gold standard of Miguel.

She'd like to say that wasn't true, but maybe it was. If truth be told, no one else's kisses had been able to turn her inside out the way Miguel's had. And on top of that, she held on to her parents' morality. She didn't like the idea of sleeping with a guy she didn't love.

And in high school, she'd loved Miguel.

Maybe a very small part of her still did.

"Well, for what it's worth," Miguel said, "I feel sorry for the real Mr. Right."

"Why is that?"

"He's going to have a rough row to hoe in pleasing your parents. Your dad might think he's a class act, but he's a real jerk."

Nicole couldn't help but smile. "After tonight, I don't blame you for feeling that way. My father wasn't exactly warm and welcoming."

"To say the least."

"When my parents finally get used to the idea and realize we're actually getting married, they'll be more accepting of you."

"So you say. But either way, I'll deal with it."

She didn't doubt that he could take it. She just wished things were different.

"But for the record," he added, "I'm glad our relationship isn't real. It would be a shame to actually be in love with you and get a reception like that from your parents."

She understood what he meant, and he was right. Yet at the same time, his words ripped into her.

Sure, they'd grown up and moved on with their lives. And their relationship was merely a business deal. But it was still a little unsettling to know that he'd stopped loving her somewhere along the way, and even more so to realize that he was glad that he had.

She glanced across the console, noting his profile, admiring the strong cut of his jaw.

The streetlight they'd parked next to provided a better glimpse of his facial features—thick eyelashes most women would die for, an aquiline nose left slightly bent after a collision with a shortstop at second base.

"Well, there's no need to sit out here all night," he said. "We may as well go inside." Then he shut off the ignition and climbed from the car.

Nicole opened the passenger door and let herself out, too. Together they walked to the front door.

There wouldn't be a good-night kiss tonight, since he'd be staying. And even though she liked the idea of sharing another heated kiss, it wasn't a good idea.

She might still have feelings for Miguel, but he'd made it clear how he felt about her.

I'm glad our relationship isn't real, he'd said just moments ago. *It would be a shame to actually be in love with you...*

So as tempting as it was to think about inviting him into her bed sometime during their make-believe engagement, it was best that she'd given him the guest room.

Even if she did let down her guard when it came to sex outside of marriage, she wouldn't sleep with a man who didn't love her.

For the next couple days, Nicole spent her evenings working late at the office. In spite of what she'd told Miguel, her reasons for doing so didn't have very much to do with the demands of her job as vice president.

In all honesty, the more time she spent away from the house, the less she had to deal with her sexy roommate. But that didn't mean she didn't think about him morning, noon and night.

How could she not? He was a real dynamo when it came to making things happen—like meeting her at the courthouse to apply for their marriage license and to line up a justice of the peace to marry them in a small, outdoor ceremony at Molly's Pride a week from Saturday.

He'd even scheduled the movers to come the day after her escrow closed. And he'd contacted the utility companies, too.

Miguel was going to make a wonderful husband one of these days. That is, if he ever decided to marry someone for real—and for keeps.

But he hadn't just hung out at the condo all day, waiting for Nicole to come home and trying to make himself useful. He'd also been talking to his cousin, Roberto Mendoza, who was a contractor and real estate developer. Together they'd been checking out sites for the nightclub he planned to open, too.

Last night, after she returned home from the office, they'd talked about it. And now that the weekend had rolled around, he wanted to show her some of the properties he was considering. Of course, that would probably have to wait until Sunday. She was having lunch at Isabella's today.

After showering, she dressed for the day, choosing a yellow sundress and a pair of low heels—something suitable for an afternoon spent at the Fortunes' ranch. Then she went into the kitchen, where she found Miguel wearing only a pair of gray sweatpants.

He'd just brewed a pot of coffee and he was placing a sliced bagel into the toaster. But any thoughts of caffeine or food slipped her mind completely as she studied his broad shoulders, his narrow waist.

As if sensing her presence, he turned to face her, his chest bare, his abs well-defined, his belly taut.

He offered her a heartwarming smile. "Good morning. How about some coffee?"

In terms of morning stimulation, caffeine was the last thing she needed. But she shook off the arousing effects of having Mr. Tall, Dark and Gorgeous in her kitchen. "Coffee sounds good. Thanks."

Miguel turned back to the carafe on the counter and reached into the cupboard for a white mug. After filling it nearly to the brim, he handed it to her. "How'd you sleep?"

"All right. And you?"

"I can't complain."

She pulled the nonfat instant creamer from the pantry, as well as the sweetener, and doctored her morning brew just the way she liked it.

As she did so, he filled a cup for himself. She took a seat at the table, assuming he'd join her. Instead, he remained standing at the kitchen counter.

"What time are you going to Isabella's?" he asked.

"I thought I'd leave at eleven-thirty, although I should probably go sooner. I'm not exactly sure how to get there."

"I'll give you directions. It's pretty easy to find. Are you nervous about having lunch with my sister?"

"No, not at all. I've always liked her. And she was really sweet when I saw her again at Red the other night. Besides, I'm looking forward to seeing Molly's Pride. A while back, I saw a photo spread and read an article in *Southwestern Ranches and Estates* about the big remodel."

She'd also been impressed by what she'd learned about the happily married couple and the amazing home they'd created together.

The toaster popped, and Miguel reached into the cupboard for a small plate. "How about a bagel?" he asked.

"You go ahead. I'll take the next one."

He nodded, then as he reached for the butter, he said,

"Molly's Pride was pretty cool when J.R. first bought it, but together, he and Isabella made it a showcase."

"That's what I gathered."

"Funny thing," Miguel said, as he turned back to face her again. "If you would have known J.R. a few years back, you never would have expected him to be the kind of guy to take up ranching."

"What do you mean?"

"I mean, he's a Fortune." Miguel leaned a hip against the kitchen counter and took a sip of his coffee. "Some of his family might be from Red Rock, but William Fortune, Jr., otherwise known as J.R., grew up in Los Angeles. He used to be a successful business exec at Fortune Forecasting, a company that specializes in predicting marketplace trends. But he gave it all up—the big-city life, designer suits and fancy coffee—to become a rancher."

"Did your sister have anything to do with that decision?"

Miguel chuckled. "No, J.R. made that move on his own. He did set his sights on her first, but she's proud of her Tejano heritage and had wanted a man who shared her same culture. So she fought her attraction to him until it was too strong to ignore."

Nicole had enjoyed reading the article and learning all about Isabella's talent. She was not only an interior designer, she was also an artist who wove the most amazing southwestern blankets and tapestries. And she had used her designing skill, as well as her artwork, to create an amazing home that reflected her heritage.

"I might ask your sister if she's interested in a decorating job," Nicole said. "I'd been meaning to hire someone to help me with the new house, but I hadn't gotten around to it yet."

"I'm sure she'd not only like working with you, but she'll also have some good ideas for you to consider." Miguel took another drink of his coffee. "You might want to discuss the wedding with her, too."

"There really isn't much to discuss. I want to keep it simple. Just our immediate family—and Marnie, of course."

"That works for me." He reached for another bagel, sliced it in half, and placed it in the toaster.

"This one's for you," he said.

"Thank you."

She studied him a moment, leaning against the kitchen counter in a cocky James Dean stance. Or maybe it wasn't so much cocky as relaxed, in control. "Thanks again for helping me coordinate all this," she said.

"My pleasure. But are you sure you want to keep things simple? I mean, most women want their wedding to be special, even if it's small—and quick. We could have a church wedding, followed by a reception at Molly's Pride."

"I couldn't possibly get married in a church when the whole thing is a sham. It wouldn't be right."

"None of this is *right,* Nicole."

She wished she had an argument, but she didn't. Her wedding day ought to be a happy occasion, one filled with love and dreams of the future—just as Marnie's wedding day would be. But she wouldn't dwell on the what-ifs.

Instead, she got up and went to the refrigerator in search of some cream cheese to spread on her bagel. Then she removed a small plate from the cupboard and waited for the toaster to pop up.

In the meantime, Miguel refilled his cup, carried it to the table and took a seat. "Have you thought about looking for a wedding dress yet?"

She bit down on her bottom lip. She probably ought to give some thought to what she'd wear, but her heart wasn't in it. Not like Marnie's was. Not when her wedding wouldn't mean the same thing.

"I'm so busy at work I'm not sure when I'd find time to shop," she said. "But I bought a white silk sundress last summer and haven't worn it yet. That would probably work for a simple outdoor ceremony."

When the toaster popped, she reached for the hot bagel and quickly transferred it to her plate.

"So what do your parents have to say about your wedding plans?" he asked.

She paused a beat, then answered truthfully. "You know, after having dinner with them, I'm not sure if I even want them to come."

"No kidding?" Miguel furrowed his brow.

"I know that I told them they could attend, but I haven't told them a day or time."

"Why not?"

"Because they're not being very supportive. Besides,

if we really had gotten back together in New York, if we'd fallen in love all over again, I would have been terribly offended by their attitudes the other night. And I wouldn't have included them. A wedding should be a happy occasion, and they would put a real damper on it."

"Hmm."

"What?" she asked, turning her back to the bagel on the counter and crossing her arms. "You don't agree?"

"Oh, I'm not questioning how you might have reacted had we actually renewed our relationship. But I was just wondering if that's the real reason."

"What do you mean?"

"Are you afraid to have them there because you might back out if they voiced their disapproval?"

"Don't be silly. If they come around, I'll include them. I just want the day to be stress-free."

She turned around, reached for the cream cheese and spread a layer on her bagel. But she didn't return to the table. Instead, she ate it while standing at the counter.

She didn't dwell on the fact that she preferred to maintain a distance. And that a full mouth made it easier not to talk about her parents anymore.

Miguel didn't comment, either, which was just as well.

As much as Nicole would like to focus on the lunch she would have with Isabella today, she couldn't help thinking about the small ceremony planned for next Saturday afternoon, as well as the people who'd be coming to wish her and Miguel well.

If her parents hadn't forced her hand, things wouldn't

have come to this. Sadly, she'd had no other choice. She either would have to go ahead with the wedding, or she would lose control of the company.

And she'd couldn't—wouldn't—let that happen.

Not when Castleton Boots was rightfully hers.

At a quarter to eleven, armed with the directions Miguel had given her to Molly's Pride, Nicole drove out to J.R. and Isabella's ranch. She was surprised at how easy it was to find—and even more so to see four cars parked in the yard.

That's odd, she thought. She'd called Isabella to confirm their lunch date on Thursday. Surely she hadn't forgotten and scheduled something else.

Then again, maybe J.R. had invited friends over.

After parking and getting out of her Lexus, Nicole scanned the rustic ranch house, its adobe brick showing under aged white stucco. According to the article she'd read, the two-hundred-year-old hacienda had once been known as the Marshall homestead before J.R. had purchased it. But these days, everyone knew it as Molly's Pride.

She made her way through a baroque stone entrance with a Moorish-style arch and up to a solid wooden door that appeared to have been handcrafted a century or more ago. She took a minute to study the carpentry of the obvious antique, then rang the bell.

Moments later, Isabella invited her inside the lovely old home, with its white plaster walls, dark wood-beam ceiling and distressed hardwood floors.

Nicole marveled at a beautiful tapestry that hung in the entry. "That's amazing. Did you make it?"

"Yes, I did."

Nicole had never been a huge fan of the southwestern style, at least for herself, but she really liked what Isabella had done with the decor.

As Miguel's sister led Nicole into a spacious living room, where several colorful woven rugs graced the distressed wood flooring, she said, "I hope you don't mind, but I thought it would be nice if you had the chance to meet some of the other women in the family. So I invited my sisters-in-law and my cousin's wife to join us today."

Nicole would have preferred a quiet lunch for two, but she couldn't very well object. So she said, "That was thoughtful. Thank you."

Isabella stopped before an attractive brunette who wore a blue-and-green gypsy skirt and matching tank top.

"This is Wendy," Isabella said. "She's one of the Atlanta Fortunes and is married to my brother Marcos."

Nicole returned the pretty woman's smile. "It's nice to meet you. Miguel and I ran into Marcos at Red the other night."

Wendy, who spoke with a slight southern drawl, said, "Marcos told me that you two were getting married. Congratulations. I hope you'll be as happy as we are."

Isabella added, "Wendy and Marcos have the cutest baby girl. Her name is MaryAnne."

"She's definitely a doll baby," Wendy said. "She's

brought so much joy to our lives. But she sure keeps us hopping."

Isabella placed a hand on her flat tummy. "I can't wait for our little one to keep us hopping."

"You're pregnant?" Nicole asked. "Miguel didn't tell me."

Isabella smiled. "He doesn't know. We've been trying for quite a while, and about the time we'd started talking about adoption… Well, J.R. and I just found out for sure yesterday."

"Congratulations," Nicole said.

"Thank you." Isabella smiled, then moved on to the next woman, a slender redhead with long, straight hair and hazel eyes. She wasn't wearing much makeup, just a light coat of lipstick, but she really didn't need more than that. She had a natural beauty—and a warm smile.

"This is Leah," Isabella said. "She's married to my brother Javier."

Nicole had heard that Javier had nearly died from injuries he'd received when the tornado struck Red Rock on New Year's Day last year. And that he'd married one of his nurses.

"I've looked forward to meeting you," Leah said. "We're happy for Miguel—and we're glad he's back home for good."

Next Isabella introduced Nicole to Melina, an attractive blonde with blue eyes who was married to Rafe. "Melina is an occupational therapist," Isabella added.

After meeting her future sisters-in-law, Nicole turned

to the last woman in the room, a breathtakingly beautiful blonde.

"And this is Frannie," Isabella said. "She was a Fortune before marrying our cousin, Roberto, a few years back."

Roberto, a local contractor and real estate developer, had been helping Miguel find the right property for his nightclub. So it was nice to meet his wife.

"We're so glad to meet you," Frannie said. "And we're happy to have you in the family."

Nicole didn't know what to say, particularly in light of her history with Miguel. Not that she didn't appreciate the warm reception, but deep down she knew she didn't deserve it.

Unlike the other women, who had been blessed with new babies and loving husbands, her own upcoming marriage wouldn't last.

"Now that our guest of honor is here," Isabella said, "let's go out to the patio for lunch."

As the women filed out of the living room, Frannie drew Nicole aside. "I meant what I said earlier. I'm so glad you and Miguel found each other again. Roberto and I were high school sweethearts, too. And we finally got back together after a fifteen-year separation."

Frannie might think they had a lot in common, but they really didn't. Okay, so they'd both fallen in love as teenagers. But Nicole and Miguel's relationship hadn't stood the test of time.

Miguel's love for her had faded.

Hers for him had faded, too, she supposed, but not

completely. The more time they spent together as adults, the more they pretended to have those same feelings, the more…well, the more confusing it all seemed.

"My mother went to unimaginable lengths to keep me and Roberto apart," Frannie added. "She even faked the results of a paternity test and orchestrated my marriage to another man."

Nicole's heart dropped to the pit of her stomach. As bad as her parents had been, as narrow-minded and demanding, she knew they never would have gone to that extreme. "That must have been devastating to learn."

"My mom has been troubled for a long time. I'm just glad that I finally learned the truth. After eighteen years, I learned that Josh, my son, was actually Roberto's child. And that Roberto had never stopped loving me."

Nicole had once believed that the love she and Miguel had felt for each other would never die, but that hadn't been the case. As romantic as it might seem to think that they'd found each other and fallen in love all over again, things hadn't worked out that way.

"It took a tragedy to get us back together," Frannie said. "It's great that you and Miguel were able to reunite on your own."

Actually, if Nicole hadn't gone to New York to beg— and to bribe—Miguel to return to Red Rock and marry her under false pretenses, they'd still be living their own lives.

"It's tough falling in love with someone your family doesn't approve of," Frannie added. "And I hope it's different for you this time around, that your parents realize how much you both care for each other."

"They're still not happy about it," Nicole admitted.

"I'm sorry to hear that. Maybe, with time, they'll come to realize they were wrong."

Poor Frannie had no idea that there was no chance of that happening. With time, Nicole and Miguel would be divorced. And her parents would think they'd been right all along. But that was her secret—hers and Miguel's.

"I hope you're right," Nicole said.

Frannie placed a hand on Nicole's arm. "Me, too. But even if your parents never accept Miguel, I can promise you that the Mendoza family will give you our unconditional love and support."

Nicole's stomach clenched. What would Miguel's family say when they learned that the marriage wasn't going to last?

While she ought to be thrilled and encouraged by Frannie's pep talk, it actually made her feel worse—about the lie she was forced to tell, about the disappointment she was sure to cause Miguel's family, who'd known how her teenage romance had ended—and who'd still welcomed her back to the fold with open arms.

At one time, she'd thought a marriage of convenience would be a win-win situation for everyone involved.

But now, as she headed out to Isabella's patio, where colorful fabrics draped a table set for six, she approached the women who'd so graciously accepted her as a sister and a wave of nausea threatened to ruin her appetite.

She wished there was another way for her to secure her position at Castleton Boots, a way that didn't force her to live a lie.

Or better yet, she wished that whatever she and Miguel had once felt for each other still burned brightly.

Chapter Six

While Nicole was having lunch with Isabella, Miguel drove into town to meet with Roberto at the old Winslow building, one of several properties he was considering and the one he liked best. He hoped Roberto could give him an idea about how much it would cost to make the necessary renovations.

"I'm sorry for being late," Roberto said upon arriving. "And unfortunately, I can't stay. I have a crew working on a project on the south side of town, and I just got a call from the foreman. One of the guys running a backhoe hit a water main, so I have to run. But I can give you a detailed estimate within the next couple days."

"You saw the inside of the building when you first

showed me the property," Miguel said. "Can you give me a ballpark figure?"

"Probably around fifty grand—maybe more. But you'll get the family discount."

"Thanks, I appreciate that."

With all he'd saved so far and the money Nicole had offered him, the plan seemed feasible.

Neither of the other two places he was considering would need as much work, but the Winslow building had a better location. And there was room to negotiate on the price based upon the money he had to put into it.

After Roberto left, Miguel hung out on Main Street for a while. Then, before running the errands he had to do while he was in town, he stopped off at Red for lunch.

"Will that be a table for one?" the hostess asked.

"No. There's a baseball game on the television in the lounge, so I'll eat in there."

The lunch crowd had already left, so the bar was nearly empty. Miguel took one of the middle bar stools, ordered a couple tacos and a Corona with lime. Then he settled into his seat and caught the score. The Rangers were down by two at the top of the fifth, but the bases were loaded, and they'd called in a pinch hitter.

Ten minutes and three runs later, the bartender brought the tacos and set the plate in front of him. "Can I get you another beer?"

"No," Miguel said, "this is plenty. Thanks."

The bartender nodded toward a doorway. "Then, if

you don't mind, I'm going into the storeroom to check inventory before the happy hour crowd shows up."

"No problem." Miguel had no more than returned his focus to the television screen when his brother's voice sounded behind him.

"Hey, I heard you snuck in here."

Miguel glanced over his shoulder as Marcos approached. "I thought I'd catch the end of the Rangers' game. They were down, but they're back on top now."

"Good." Marcos placed his forearm on the empty stool next to Miguel. He watched the next batter strike out, then said, "I assume Nicole is out at Molly's Pride with the other women."

"The *other* women?"

"Isabella invited Wendy, Melina and Leah to join them for lunch. I think Frannie went, too."

Miguel wondered how Nicole would feel about that. She hadn't been expecting an afternoon with the girls.

"You look surprised," Marcos said.

"I guess I shouldn't be. It only stands to reason that the women in the family would be curious about Nicole and eager to learn more about the wedding."

"It's not just the women who are curious," Marcos said. "The whole family knew how you felt about each other back in high school."

But no one more than Marcos, Miguel supposed.

"I hope this time around things work out."

Miguel shot a glance at his brother, saw the question in his eyes. "Don't worry. I'm not going to get hurt."

Marcos paused for a beat, then seemed to shake off

whatever concern he might have had. "I'm sure you won't."

"What about the others? Are they putting too much stock in the way things ended last time?"

"I don't think so. We're glad you finally got back together. In fact, we've all been a little worried about you over the years, so we're relieved to see that you're finally going to settle down."

"You've been worried about *me?*" Miguel took a sip of his beer, then set the bottle aside. "Why?"

"Because you've always played the part of the happy-go-lucky bachelor, but I figured you were actually on the run."

"On the run? From what?"

"Love, commitment, heartbreak. You name it. Ever since you split up with Nicole, you've had your guard up and wouldn't let other women get too close."

"Yeah, well, that's crazy. I've been over Nicole for years."

"You've been *over* her?" Marcos arched a brow, picking up on the slip of tongue.

Now what?

Miguel hadn't meant to tip his hand. But it wasn't going to be easy to lie to Marcos now, especially since they'd always had an honest relationship. So he scanned the lounge, making sure there wasn't anyone within earshot.

When he realized their conversation would be private, he lowered his voice anyway and pointed to the bar stool on which Marcos was resting his arm. "Take some of the weight off your feet."

Miguel waited for Marcos to pull out the stool and sit down, then he told him about Nicole's visit to New York, about the business deal they'd made.

Disbelief stretched across his brother's face. "No kidding?"

Miguel shrugged. "With the money she offered me for going along with it, I can open that nightclub a lot sooner than I'd planned. In fact, I've been looking at property in the downtown area and found a couple places I think will work, one in particular."

"You mean that whole romantic dinner and public proposal was fake?" Marcos grew silent, his brow furrowed.

"What's the matter?" Miguel asked.

"It's not right, man."

Miguel sighed. "I know. I wish Nicole would have told her parents to take a flying leap, then marched out of the office and disappeared for a few weeks. They would have backed down and turned the company over to her. After all, they think she walks on water. But she didn't agree. She said they'd backed her into a corner with no other way out."

"I don't care what she tells her parents. What about *your* family? We've always been supportive of you and anything you choose to do. And you're deceiving all of us, too."

"I'm not happy about that. But we're going through

with the wedding. And for as long as it lasts, it'll be real in every sense of the word."

At least that was the game plan. And it was the reason he could deceive his family without feeling an unbearable amount of guilt.

"So you're going to marry a woman you claim you no longer love?" Marcos asked.

"That's about the size of it." Miguel might still feel something for Nicole, but it wasn't love. Couldn't be.

On the other hand, their chemistry was as strong and hot as before and was another story altogether.

"How long do you think a marriage that's nothing more than a business deal is going to last?"

"Down the road, after she takes control of Castleton Boots, we'll get a divorce. But either way, the split will be amicable. No one will get hurt, and neither family will be affected, as long as we keep this to ourselves."

"So you say."

"What do you mean by that?"

Marcos clucked his tongue. "The rest of the family might not have known it, but I did. You were pretty torn up by that split. And while you say you've got things under control, I'm still not so sure. You might be risking your heart again."

For a moment, Miguel considered the truth in his brother's words. But he shook it off and managed an easy grin. "I'm not a kid anymore. I know what I'm doing."

"Okay, but it still feels wrong to me."

"It's a job—a business arrangement. A means to an end for both of us."

Marcos leaned forward, his gaze locking on Miguel's. "Okay, but I'm not buying that you're only doing this for the money. I think you still have feelings for her. And I know how hard you took your first breakup. You went so far as to convince Mom and Dad to let you finish school in Mexico so you wouldn't have to face Nicole each day. So you can't blame me for worrying about you—and about how you'll handle a split after investing your time with her now."

"Easy. When it's done, we'll both go our own way."

"Just like that?"

Miguel released his hold on his longneck beer bottle and snapped his fingers. "Just like that." He narrowed his gaze as if insisting he was telling the truth, although a niggle of doubt elbowed him in the ribs. But he didn't pay it any heed. He might have loved Nicole once, but that was a long time ago.

Marcos studied him a moment, then said, "She's a beautiful woman."

"I can't argue that." Miguel glanced at the television screen in an attempt to escape his brother's assessment.

"And you moved in with her?" Marcos asked.

"Into her guest room. We thought it would make things more believable if people thought we were living together."

"That public proposal in the courtyard the other night certainly looked like the real deal, especially when you kissed her. How long do you think you'll stay in that guest room?"

Not much longer, if Miguel had his way, but he kept that to himself.

Some things should remain private—like a man's plan to sweep his future bride off her feet, to remind her how good their lovemaking had once been and to suggest that they become business partners with benefits.

Before leaving the ranch and heading home, Leah, Melina, Wendy and Frannie each embraced Nicole and wished her the best.

"We'll see you at the wedding next Saturday," Wendy said, "if not before."

Isabella walked with her guests to the front door and told them goodbye.

Before Nicole could follow the others outside, Isabella stopped her. "Let's take some time to discuss the wedding details."

"All right," Nicole said. "But don't forget that we really want to keep things small and simple."

"No problem. Come with me." Isabella closed the front door, then walked Nicole through the house and out a side door that opened to a lovely courtyard adorned with lush hanging plants bursting with colorful flowers. In the center was a remarkable water fountain with red, yellow and purple ceramic tile that appeared to have been handcrafted by artisans.

"What do you think?" Isabella asked. "We can have

the justice of the peace stand near the potted hibiscus that's by the far wall."

"That works for me."

"Good. I'll call the party rental company and have them bring out chairs. We can arrange them so there's an aisle for you to walk down."

At the mention of "party" and "guests," Nicole stiffened. "We'll really only need seating for a few people."

"I hope you're not limiting the guest list on our behalf. J.R. and I don't mind how many people you invite. You must have coworkers and business associates you'll want to include."

"No, not really. If we didn't need a witness or two, we'd probably elope."

"I'm not trying to pressure you," Isabella said. "It's your special day. Whatever you want is fine. J.R. and I are happy to be a part of it and to help in any way we can."

"Thank you for understanding. We're only inviting immediate family—your father, your brothers and their wives. And my best friend, Marnie, of course."

And now that Marnie was engaged, Nicole would have to include Asher Fortune, too. Not that she had anything against the man. Asher was a great guy and the love of Marnie's life. But that just meant adding one more witness to the ceremony that joined Nicole and Miguel in phony matrimony.

"If your parents have any close friends or associates who should be included," Isabella said, "just say the word."

GET 2 BOOKS

We'd like to send you two *Harlequin® Special Edition* novels absolutely free. Accepting them puts you under no obligation to purchase any more books.

HOW TO GET YOUR 2 FREE BOOKS AND 2 FREE GIFTS

1. Return the reply card today, and we'll send you two *Harlequin Special Edition* novels, absolutely free! We'll even pay the postage!

2. Accepting free books places you under no obligation to buy anything, ever. Whatever you decide, the free books and gifts are yours to keep, free!

3. We hope that after receiving your free books you'll want to remain a subscriber, but the choice is yours—to continue or cancel, any time at all!

EXTRA BONUS

You'll also get two free mystery gifts! (worth about $10)

FREE!

Return this card today to get
2 FREE BOOKS and 2 FREE GIFTS!

HARLEQUIN®

SPECIAL EDITION

YES! Please send me 2 FREE *Harlequin® Special Edition*
novels, and 2 FREE mystery gifts as well. I understand
I am under no obligation to purchase anything, as
explained on the back of this insert.

235/335 HDL FVQW

Please Print

FIRST NAME	LAST NAME

ADDRESS

APT.#	CITY

Visit us at:
www.ReaderService.com

STATE/PROV.   ZIP/POSTAL CODE

◀ **DETACH AND MAIL CARD TODAY!** ▶

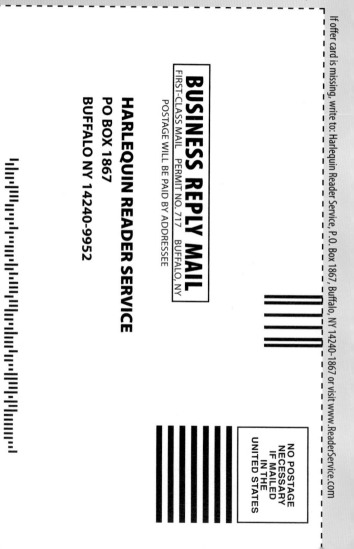

Nicole wasn't even sure she'd give the wedding details to her parents, let alone allow them to issue invitations of their own. But she certainly wouldn't mention that to Miguel's sister. "Thanks. I'll let them know."

"Great. And don't worry about letting me know at the last minute. J.R. and I wouldn't mind a bit. Besides, we both realize that you have a lot of things to do and not long to do it."

"Miguel will be a big help."

"Have you found a dress yet?" Isabella asked.

A real bride probably would consider her gown to be a priority, but Nicole hadn't put any thought to those kinds of details. And to be honest, the whole wedding was getting seriously out of hand.

Why hadn't she insisted they elope?

"I'll probably go look for a dress tomorrow," Nicole said, even though she would probably end up wearing the white silk sundress that had been hanging in her closet since last season.

Of course, if she did decide to go shopping, that would have to take place after Miguel showed her the property he intended to buy. His eyes lit up whenever he talked about the nightclub, and she liked knowing she'd played a small part in putting the spark there.

A spark he'd once had whenever he'd looked at her.

Her thoughts drifted and the memories unfolded to a simpler time, when Miguel could turn her inside out with a single glance. In fact, if he still looked at her that way, as if she were the only woman in the world, she'd be a whole lot more excited about the upcoming ceremony—and the honeymoon.

"If you want someone to go shopping with you," Isabella added, "just give me a call. I know of a few places in San Antonio that are very chic and stylish."

Under normal circumstances Nicole would have appreciated Isabella's offer, especially since Marnie was so busy with Asher these days. But it was getting more and more difficult to downplay the ceremony, especially now that Miguel's family was all on board.

"Thanks for the offer," she told Isabella, "I'd love to take you up on it, but I'm not going to waste time looking for just the right dress. I'll probably stick with something simple. Besides, I've heard that wedding gowns have to be specially ordered, and they can take months to get."

"With your shape and size, I'll bet the stores might actually have something in stock."

"Thank you. I hope you're right. And thanks again for being so supportive."

"I'm just so happy for you and Miguel."

It was too bad Nicole's mother wasn't able to share in the excitement or in the planning. But then again, what was there to be excited about?

The wedding was merely a vehicle to get her and Miguel what they both wanted.

Yet somewhere deep inside, Nicole wished that things could be different, that things could be…real.

Nicole probably should have jumped on Isabella's offer to go shopping with her, but she'd had enough wedding talk for one day.

And enough guilt.

It was no surprise that her parents had opposed the marriage, even if they'd kept relatively quiet about it, at least publicly. But the Mendozas, who'd probably known or suspected that the Castletons hadn't thought Miguel was good enough for Nicole when they'd been teenagers, could have held that against her now. Instead, they'd welcomed her into the family fold.

And she was going to disappoint them all.

At one time, Nicole had dreamed of being part of a large family—*Miguel's* family. And the fact that everyone was being so kind and accepting just made her guilt all the worse, especially when she knew how their temporary marriage arrangement would eventually turn out.

It didn't seem right to make friends with the Mendoza women only to end those relationships later.

So she'd thanked Isabella again for hosting such a lovely lunch, then climbed into her Lexus and drove back to town.

On the way home, she stopped by the market and picked up something to fix for dinner—chicken breasts, pasta and the makings for a salad. Miguel had offered to fix dinner the past few nights, but she'd told him not to bother, that she'd be working late. And while staying at the office longer than anyone else had been a habit of hers, she'd actually been avoiding having dinner alone with him. But she wouldn't use that excuse tonight.

They could, of course, go out to dinner, but that meant Nicole would have to fall into the role of a starry-

eyed bride-to-be one more time in public. And after
the last couple hours she'd spent playing the part, she
wasn't up for it.

But was she up for a quiet dinner for two with her
handsome new roommate?

She wished she could say that she was, but somewhere along the way, the business arrangement she'd
proposed had gone south.

Those renewed puppy-love feelings aside, she still
found Miguel incredibly attractive. Just being near him
stirred longings and desire she'd thought had died years
ago. And the thought of being alone with him this evening left her a little unbalanced.

The image of her plucking daisy petals came to
mind—*I want him, I want him not.*

She blew out a sigh, wishing she could blame her
parents for the mess she'd found herself in. But it wasn't
entirely their fault. After all, she'd been the one who'd
concocted the plan to marry Miguel for spite—and to
secure her position as the new CEO of Castleton Boots.

And in the process, she'd resurrected old emotions
that were better left dead and buried.

She had no idea what the next week would bring, but
she couldn't very well backpedal now. Things would
have to move forward as planned.

With that decided, she pulled into her driveway, went
into the condo and put away the groceries she wouldn't
need for tonight's dinner, setting the others on the counter. Then she marinated the chicken breasts, prepared a
salad and whipped up a homemade vinaigrette dressing.

Several times she glanced at the clock in the kitchen, wondering when Miguel would get home.

Just after five o'clock, she put some music on the stereo, something soft and soothing. Then she had second thoughts. Faith Hill and Tim McGraw duets were going to be way too romantic for the type of evening she had in mind.

Rather than change the CD to one with a livelier beat, she shut off the power and turned on the television instead.

Yet after countless rounds of channel surfing, she couldn't find a single show or movie to interest her and gave up trying. So off it went, as well.

Next she went to the front window and peered out into the street. Where was he? Shouldn't he be home by now?

Oh, for Pete's sake. She was pacing the floor—and climbing the walls. Why was she so nervous and fidgety?

Because she was getting cold feet about the wedding ceremony, even if it was just going to be a small one.

Was it too late for a change of plans now?

She and Miguel could tell Isabella that they'd been so eager to make things legal that they'd decided not to wait another week and to elope. Wasn't that what Miguel had suggested they do in the first place?

As she started back across the living room floor for what seemed to be the hundredth time, the doorknob clicked and turned. Moments later, Miguel stepped into the house carrying a large garment bag and wearing a sexy grin that left her not only unbalanced, but ready to topple over with the very next heartbeat.

Too bad she hadn't left the Faith and Tim duet playing. It certainly fit the mood right now.

But she shrugged it off and nodded toward the garment bag. "What have you got in there?"

"I thought you should have something special to wear for the wedding."

He went shopping? For *her?*

Her jaw must have dropped because his grin faded and he added, "You said you were too busy at work to go shopping—and with that lunch today and our plans to look at property tomorrow…well, I didn't think you'd have much time available this weekend."

Miguel had impeccable taste in clothing, particularly his own. So she didn't doubt the dress he'd chosen would have possibilities.

Any other female workaholic who'd made a business deal with him might have considered the cost— and offered to reimburse him, assuming whatever he'd chosen fit and was halfway stylish. But today, Nicole wasn't thinking about bottom lines or balance sheets.

"You bought a *wedding dress* for me?" she asked, amazed at how decisive and proactive he could be.

"I had to guess at the size, so I'm not sure if it'll fit. Or if you'll even like it. Why don't you try it on?"

At that, she crossed the room and met him in the middle of the floor. "I can't believe this."

"Believe what?" he asked. "Are you angry?"

"No. It's just that…" She reached out and touched

the bag, wondering what he'd chosen. "I didn't expect you to do something like this."

"You haven't seen it yet."

No, she hadn't. But the gesture was so…thoughtful, so sweet, so…completely unexpected.

"Don't get the wrong idea," he said. "I didn't start out on a shopping trip. After meeting with Roberto, I stopped by Red for lunch. And then I decided to take another look at the property. Earlier, I'd checked out the nearby restaurants, shops and businesses. But for some reason, I'd missed seeing a women's clothing store before. And yet there it was, three doors down. In the window I spotted a mannequin wearing a white dress that caught my eye."

"Was it a bridal shop?"

"No, but I figured the dress would look amazing on you. And that it was more formal than a sundress, yet still okay for a casual outdoor wedding, especially since I'll be wearing a suit. So I bought it. If you don't like it, I'll return it tomorrow." With that, he unzipped the garment bag and pulled out a sleek yet simple calf-length gown she could wear in the evenings if she were to go out on the town.

She didn't know what to say. Not only was it stylish, but it was… Well, it was just the kind of thing she might have purchased for herself—if she'd taken the time to do so.

She touched the slinky fabric, trying to imagine what it would feel like against her skin, what it would look like when she slipped it on.

"It's white and pure," Miguel said. "But yet it's classy and sexy, too. What do you think?"

She thought it was perfect. That is, assuming it fit her.

"If you don't like it, we can return it," he repeated.

She turned, eyes wide and seeking his. "Don't be silly. I love it."

"Good. Then try it on."

"Here? Now?"

"Why not? Take it into the bedroom and see how it fits. I'll wait here for you to come out."

She wanted to object, to blurt out that it was bad luck for the groom to see the bridal dress—especially on his future bride—before the wedding. But old wives' tales and superstitions probably didn't count when it came to marriages of convenience.

Besides, her luck didn't seem to be so good these days anyway.

She checked the tag—size eight. She'd have to try it on to know for sure, but it ought to fit. And Miguel had guessed that it would, just by seeing it on a mannequin?

For some dumb reason, her eyes filled with tears.

"What's wrong?" he asked. "Did you have your heart set on choosing the dress yourself?"

"No, that's not it."

Miguel took her hand and gave it a warm, gentle squeeze. "I just thought we should make everything appear authentic so that we can pull off the ruse."

One tear slipped down her cheek, followed by another. He released his hold on her hand, then reached out and ran the curve of his index finger below her eyes, catching the droplets, drying her skin.

His tender response, his gentle touch, his manly scent all worked against her, sending her heart scampering through her chest.

He was so close….

All she had to do was lift her hand to touch him, to reach behind his neck and draw his mouth to hers in a long, deep kiss.

But she couldn't possibly make a move like that.

All right, she definitely could. But she shouldn't. And she wouldn't.

One heated kiss would only lead to another, and before long, she'd want more. So much more.

Yet in spite of her resolve, her heart pounded in anticipation as the ever-present tension swirled around them, complicating everything.

All her life—well, up until she'd broken up with Miguel in high school—she'd dreamed of this day.

Okay, so not this particular day. But she'd dreamed of a time such as this one, a time when she'd be looking forward to walking down the aisle and carrying a bouquet.

Uh-oh, flowers—one more thing she'd forgotten to add to her list of things to do. She'd have to call the florist that was located near the office. That is, if she and Miguel actually went through with the wedding and didn't elope.

She looked at the dress one more time. It really was pretty. And for a moment, she envisioned Miguel standing at the altar of Red Rock Community Church, waiting for her, longing for her, loving her....

Then reality set in.

She would marry Miguel on Saturday, but that's where the perfect illusion would end. Their vows might be legal, yet the rest of it—the white dress, the tiered cake, the professions of love, the promise of forever—was merely a dream that would never come true.

Chapter Seven

Miguel sat in the living room, waiting for Nicole to come out of her bedroom and model the dress he'd purchased an hour ago. She seemed a bit skittish this evening, as if she was ready to bolt. Either that or to burst into tears again.

He'd heard that brides sometimes got emotional, but in her case, that didn't seem feasible.

Footsteps sounded in the hall, and he glanced at the doorway, watching as she swept into the room, the slinky material hugging each and every curve.

His breath caught at the sight. That mannequin had nothing on her. Hell, neither did Kate Middleton.

"What's the matter?" she asked.

He found his voice. "Nothing's wrong. It's…perfect. You look great."

"You're not just saying that, are you?"

"Absolutely not." He wouldn't lie to her, yet he still read insecurity and skepticism in her gaze.

She turned to the right, flashing him a glimpse of the lovely curve of her backside. "Does it make my butt look big?"

She was kidding, right?

When she turned around to face him, her gaze seeking some kind of confirmation, a slow smile tugged at his lips. "You've got the cutest butt I've ever seen—covered in silk or just bare skin."

They stood in silence, aware of what they'd once had and caught up in something neither of them had expected—tempted beyond reason, taunted beyond measure.

The years began to roll back, the pain and disappointments, too. And for a couple of beats, they were seventeen again, with eyes only for each other.

Without a conscious thought, Miguel reached out and skimmed his fingers along the curve of her hip, along the sleek fabric of her dress. The moment he touched her, a bolt of heat shot clean through him, and it took all he had not to scoop her into his arms and carry her to bed.

Her breath hitched and her lips parted at the sensual caress, but she didn't pull away, didn't object.

In fact, she continued to study him in silence.

He could make another seductive move, he supposed, but for some reason, he opted to wait until the time was right. Until the mood had been set.

"Do you have a passport?" he asked.

"I… Yes, I do. Why?"

"Be sure to pack it for the honeymoon."

She cocked her head slightly to the side and furrowed her brow. "You're planning a *honeymoon?*"

"Yes, ma'am." And thanks to a few strings Miguel had pulled, as well as the generosity of his buddy, Sawyer Fortune, he added, "The best one ever."

"I'm not sure that's a good idea." Her voice came out soft, low and a bit breathy.

"A honeymoon will be expected."

"Of course. You're right."

"As a side note," he added, "I realize your heart might not be in it, but I plan to make the best of this. And that means that I intend for our wedding, as well as our marriage, as short as it might be, to be real in every sense of the word."

It was also the only way he'd be able to pull off their ploy without disappointing his family—and maybe even himself.

There she went again with that slight cock of her head, that arch of a single brow.

He'd been talking about sex, and she seemed to be wrapping her mind around his intention—struggling with it, no doubt.

Good. That meant she was considering it, too.

"If you're talking about making love," she said, "that would only complicate things."

"I'm sure you're right. But in a nice way." He tossed

her a crooked grin, then turned and headed for the guest room.

He didn't doubt for a moment that his words had stunned her, tempted her. They also gave her something to think about, maybe even dream about when she climbed into bed alone.

Good. He wanted it that way.

He might need a cold shower tonight, but if things went his way—and he had no doubt they would—he wouldn't need another frigid dunking for the duration of their marriage.

If Nicole hadn't already agreed to go with Miguel on Sunday to look at the property he was considering for his nightclub, she would have found an excuse to leave the house at the crack of dawn, just so she could avoid him.

Not that she wasn't sorely tempted to let their relationship take a sexual turn. After all, she was only human. And she knew firsthand just how good making love with him would be. But she also feared the complications that would bring.

She'd told herself that she'd gotten over him years ago, but she wasn't so sure about that anymore. Either way, the attraction she felt was certainly alive and well. Last night was proof of that. He'd set her blood on fire with a single look, a single touch.

After a quiet dinner, he'd turned in early, as if thoughts of sex hadn't fazed him at all. Yet she'd lain awake for hours, dreaming of how it used to be, doubting if a platonic marriage would work with her paired up with Miguel and wondering if he was right about making things as real as they could be, under the circumstances.

Finally morning came. After a cup of coffee and a light breakfast, they took her car into town.

"It's not much on the outside," he warned, as she turned down Main Street. "But keep in mind that Roberto and I are going to remodel it."

He told her to take the parking space in front of an ugly orange-and-brown building, a crack in the front window.

"This is it," he said, as he got out of the car. "What do you think?"

"It's going to need a lot of work—starting with several coats of paint."

"Absolutely. And all-new outdoor lighting, as well as a big neon sign that says Mendoza's. You won't recognize it when we're finished."

Nicole tried to envision the abandoned building as a country-western nightclub, a place where the locals would hang out and kick up their heels.

"I wish I could take you inside," he said, leading her to a dirt-smudged window, his voice sparked with enthusiasm. "You'll have to use your imagination for now. Picture hardwood floors and one of those old-style cowboy bars all along the east wall, the kind a thirsty, fun-loving cowboy can belly up to. But the rest of it will be modern, with large screens playing country music videos when a band isn't on the stage. There's also going to be a raised dance floor."

He was right. The building itself wasn't much on the outside, but the location was perfect. And it was certainly large enough for what he had in mind.

She stole a glance at her old high school boyfriend as he peered through the window. She caught the glimmer in his eye, the smile that ran far deeper than the surface.

She was glad she'd come, glad he'd shared this moment with her. His excitement, especially since she'd known how long he'd dreamed of owning a nightclub, was contagious, filling her own heart and soul with all the possibilities.

He turned to her and asked, "So what do you really think?"

She knew he'd make up his own mind, that he'd go to Roberto for advice, if he thought he needed it. Yet it pleased her to know that her opinion somehow mattered.

"You've found a jewel," she said.

His smile broadened. "I'm glad you like it. I'm meeting with Roberto this afternoon. As long as the numbers work out, we'll try to negotiate a lease with an option to buy. The owner died about a year ago, and the place was tied up in probate. A nephew has control of it now, and according to Roberto, he lives out of state and just wants to unload it."

"Good luck."

"Thanks."

Their gazes met, and for a moment, she felt a connection form between them. Or had she only imagined it?

"Would you like to stop by Red for lunch?" he asked.

A chicken tostada actually sounded good, but she feared she might lose her head around him. So she needed to put a little space between the two of them until the wedding on Saturday.

"I'd better not," she said. "I have to go into the office today. I have a meeting early tomorrow morning, and I'm not ready for it."

If he suspected she was lying, he didn't comment. But then again, maybe he was just too focused on the lease, on the remodel and the nightclub he planned to open sometime this summer. And if so, that was just as well.

It made tiptoeing around a sexual relationship that much easier.

On Monday morning, Nicole left the house early for the office, reminding Miguel about the meeting she'd told him she had to attend. And while there hadn't been any such meeting, that didn't mean she couldn't find plenty of things to do that would serve to keep her mind off her handsome houseguest.

And that's just what she did.

Two hours later, she was knee-deep in researching a question the CPA had asked over the telephone earlier today when her father came into her office. On some level she sensed his presence, but she didn't look up from the paperwork on her desk until he cleared his throat.

Instead of the warm, jovial greeting she usually received, his demeanor was stiff, his arms crossed.

"Have you been avoiding your mother and me?" he asked.

She often found herself guarding her answers to his questions, especially when her father was so direct. But this time she opted for honesty—at least, as much as she dared. "In a way, I suppose I have been keeping to myself. Things were pretty stressful when we had dinner at the country club last week. And I didn't want to put Miguel through another evening like that."

Her father clucked his tongue. "I don't know what you're talking about. Under the circumstances, your mother and I were more than cordial. You can't blame us for not liking the idea of you marrying a man you hardly even know. And don't tell me you've known each other for years. That's bunk. You were kids back then, and you've both changed."

She pushed her chair away from her desk and stood. "Well, I'm not a kid anymore, Daddy. And neither is Miguel. I can look out for myself. I'm a college graduate—and I'm a respected member of the Castleton Boots team."

"Of course you are. All I'm asking is that you not do anything hasty."

"Like what?" she asked, knowing full well what he meant.

"If you're planning to marry that man just so you can gain control of the company, you'll be making a big mistake. It's not too late for me to make changes. I can leave everything to the Red Rock Humane Society if I want to."

"The only reason I'm marrying Miguel is because I love him," Nicole said. "End of story."

She crossed her own arms at that point, wishing her words were true. Then she added, "If you and Mom hadn't interfered last time, you might have been grandparents already. As it is, you'll have to wait until we get around to planning a family."

She probably ought to tell her father that she and Miguel were getting married at Molly's Pride next Saturday at one o'clock, but she couldn't quite bring herself to do it. In fact, there had to be a hundred reasons why she kept dragging her feet, only one of which was their attitude toward Miguel.

The past and old hurts came into play, too.

When her mom and dad had learned that she and Miguel were having sex, they'd flipped out. She supposed she could understand that. But they'd refused to consider her feelings and insisted that she break up with him, threatening to send her off to boarding school if she didn't.

She'd gone along with their wishes, like the obedient daughter she'd always tried her best to be.

Still, they'd placed a curfew on her until she'd left for college, demanding that she be home each night by nine.

She supposed they had assumed teenagers wouldn't have sex or couldn't get into trouble during the daylight hours.

Yet even now, ten years later, she sensed that they still didn't trust her to do the right thing without their guidance. So at twenty-seven, she'd finally begun to rebel—at least, passively.

That's why she'd purchased the new house and planned to move away from the gated community where they lived. That's also why she flew to New York and offered to pay Miguel to marry her.

And that's why she wouldn't mention the wedding to her parents until after the ink had dried on the license.

The rest of the week went by in a blur, and before Nicole knew it, Saturday dawned warm and bright. As she lay in bed alone, she realized how little she had seen of her handsome houseguest the past few days. And while she'd started out doing everything she could to avoid crossing his path, it hadn't taken much effort once he'd cinched the deal on the Winslow building.

Last Tuesday morning he had signed a five-year lease with an option to buy, and from then on, he'd left the house just after sunrise and didn't return until after dark. They'd hardly seen each other since.

She had a feeling that's what she could expect from their short-lived marriage. Miguel would spend nights and weekends working at the nightclub, and she'd be at the office from Monday through Friday.

I can see where that will create problems on the home front, her father had said while they'd had dinner at the country club. *What kind of life is that for a man who expects to have a happy wife and family?*

He'd had a point, she supposed. But theirs wasn't going to be a traditional marriage. It was merely a way for them to each make their dreams come true. Miguel was getting the nightclub he'd always wanted, and she'd soon be the CEO of Castleton Boots.

Don't worry about the time Miguel will need to spend away from home, Nicole had told her father that night. And it's what she reminded herself now. They'd work things out—one way or another.

Nicole glanced at the clock on the bureau. It was already after eight o'clock—her wedding day had finally dawned. So she threw off the covers and climbed out of bed.

After a stretch and a yawn, she padded to the bedroom window, opened the shutters and peered outside, where gray clouds greeted her instead of sunny blue skies.

An omen? she wondered.

She shook off the superstitious thought, choosing to be more practical instead. What would they do if it rained?

Move the ceremony into the ranch house, she supposed.

After showering, she used a blow-dryer to style her hair to a soft, glossy shine. Then she applied some lipstick and slipped on a pair of white jeans and a turquoise blouse.

Next she packed the rest of her makeup in an overnight bag, as well as her brush and curling iron. She left the dress hanging in the closet until it was time to drive to the ranch, where she would get dressed for the wedding.

She also packed a couple outfits in her suitcase and placed her passport in her purse. Miguel had mentioned them going on a honeymoon, but he was so caught up in renovations and the remodel that she doubted he'd want to leave town. Either way, he couldn't say that she dropped the ball.

It was nearly ten when she went to the kitchen, where a gorgeous, barefoot Miguel stood at the counter, wearing a pair of worn denim jeans and a black tank shirt. He was pouring what had to be his second or third cup of coffee, since the carafe was nearly empty.

He turned when she entered, scanned the length of her, then flashed her a dazzling smile. "Good morning. Are you ready for the big day?"

As ready as she'd ever be, she supposed. She offered him a smile and nodded.

"Are you packed?" he asked.

"Almost. But I thought I'd better ask if you still planned to take time off for a honeymoon."

He leaned his hip against the counter. "Why wouldn't I?"

"Because of all the work you have to do on the building."

"I spent the past few days getting everything and everyone lined out. There's no reason why I can't leave town now. Do you have your passport?"

"Yes, I packed some basic essentials, but I wasn't sure what else I'd need. You haven't told me where we're going."

"It's a surprise. But I will say that you'll probably

want to take a swimsuit or two. Maybe some shorts, a sundress, some sandals. And speaking of surprises, I invited a friend to the wedding."

She tried to think of all the guys he'd known in school. Was he still close to any of them?

"Who'd you invite?" she asked. "Do I know him?"

"I don't think so. It's Sawyer Fortune. I just met him a year and a half ago, but we hit it off immediately. Besides, I owed him an invitation to my wedding."

Nicole had met several of the Fortunes at charity events over the years, but Sawyer hadn't been one of them. While she wasn't happy about adding any extra people to the wedding guest list, she was curious about the man, about the friendship he had with Miguel. "So where'd you meet him?"

Miguel chuckled. "I guess you could say we met at Marcos and Wendy's wedding, although it was actually in the bar while watching ESPN on television and drinking beer. I never have enjoyed attending weddings and receptions, especially when they interfered with sporting events. So I slipped off to check out the score of the Cowboys game, only to find an Atlanta Falcons fan doing the same thing."

"And that was Sawyer?"

"Yep. It didn't take long to learn that, even though we favored different teams to make the playoffs, we had a lot in common."

"Such as...?"

"Well, we were both dyed-in-the-wool bachelors who'd rather be anywhere else than at a wedding reception. We're about the same age. We lived out of state at the time, had family in Red Rock and knew some of the same people. We also liked sports—baseball, football, you name it."

"How'd you maintain a relationship while living in New York?"

"We got involved in a fantasy football league and kept in contact through email. He's back in Red Rock now. I ran into him yesterday, so I told him about the wedding."

"What did you guys do? Make some kind of bet about who'd be the first to give up his freedom?"

"It was more like an agreement that we'd never get married. And that if we did, the other would get a front row seat and bragging rights. I hope you don't mind. Sawyer's a great guy. I think you'll like him. Most women do."

It sounded as though the two bachelors did have a lot in common, because Miguel was one handsome man— and charming to boot. There'd be plenty of women disappointed when they learned he was off the market. And he would be, at least temporarily.

Maybe she should have made some kind of dating stipulation in their agreement. She wouldn't like it if he immediately jumped back into his footloose bachelor lifestyle the moment they filed for divorce.

She didn't offer a comment, only a smile as she removed the nonfat creamer from the pantry and placed a spoonful into her coffee.

The wedding guest list had now grown to a whopping fourteen, not counting the justice of the peace or the bride and groom.

"Did you decide to invite your parents to the wedding after all?" Miguel asked.

Actually, it had crossed her mind a couple times, but she didn't want to mar the day with their negativity, their stiff and flawed attempts to appear polite. Especially when the Mendozas had been amazingly supportive.

Besides, Miguel, who'd been so sweet, didn't deserve their haughty expressions.

"No," she said. "If we'd run off to Las Vegas, they would have missed seeing the actual ceremony anyway."

"I still think you should tell them and give them the option of attending or not."

Why should they witness a wedding that wasn't for the right reasons?

And why would Miguel care anyway?

"As a side note," he added, "it would serve them right to see us tie the knot and not be able to stop it from happening this time around."

It would "serve them right"? Maybe so. But had he agreed to marry her for more reasons than money?

Her heart clenched at the thought. After she'd first offered to pay him when she'd met him for dinner in New York, he'd turned her down. It wasn't until he'd had time to reconsider that he'd changed his mind.

She tried to read his expression, but wasn't having much luck.

As if noting her curiosity, he shrugged. "I really don't care one way or the other. It was just a suggestion."

Nicole had no reason not to believe him. Yet she still felt a little uneasy because of his comment, as well as the thought of inviting her parents.

She supposed he had a point, but who knew what kind of pall her father—if not her mother—would cast over the otherwise happy event.

Still, the more people who witnessed the vows, the more traditional the wedding seemed.

And the more Nicole questioned her decision to exclude her mom and dad.

Chapter Eight

J.R. and Isabella's courtyard had always held a quaint charm, but the recent renovations they'd made—the new water fountain that gurgled in the center of the walled yard and the lush hanging plants and pots of flowers placed throughout—created a peaceful setting in which to gather for a wedding.

Miguel, who stood next to his brother Marcos and the justice of the peace, scanned the smiling faces of his other family members who waited for the ceremony to begin.

The rented chairs on which they now sat had been covered in fancy white fabric and bows and set up in two rows of eight, with a short aisle down the middle.

Just moments ago, Andy and Elizabeth Castleton had arrived at the ranch. Earlier this morning, Miguel had encouraged Nicole to call and extend a late invitation, and she had. He looked forward to having them there, to seeing their reaction when their daughter married the guy they'd believed was beneath her.

Okay, so maybe there was a small part of him that still hoped that they'd finally accept him, that he might even win them over. But that wasn't likely.

Either way, Miguel had told Nicole that her parents' absence would have been difficult to explain to his family, who'd turned out in full support.

Of course, it wouldn't take anyone long to connect a few of the dots, if they hadn't done so already, and realize that the Castletons would rather be getting root canals than have front-row seats at the wedding. Not while Andy sat as stiff as a Buckingham Palace guard, and Elizabeth dabbed at her eyes with a linen handkerchief.

Some might think their presence made things awkward—and for Nicole, it probably had. But Miguel still took a bit of pleasure in knowing that they hadn't been able to stop the wedding.

Of course, he still wished that Nicole would have told them what they could do with their legal stipulations and the stock they held in front of her like carrots. Instead she'd chosen a more passive way to rebel.

And what if she had? He still intended to make the best of their short marriage, and that meant whisking his wife off on a romantic honeymoon that he'd not only planned but paid for.

They might have made a business arrangement, for

which he was being financially compensated, but he wouldn't let her call all the shots—or pay for them.

Across the aisle, Luis Mendoza, Miguel's father, sat front and center, wearing a happy smile and looking dapper in his new gray suit. He turned and whispered something to Isabella and J.R., who were seated next to him.

Behind them, Wendy, Marcos's wife, as well as Asher Fortune, Marnie's fiancé, sat together.

Leah and Javier, plus Rafe and Melina, filled the other chairs, their smiles, occasional nods and whispers evidence of their unconditional acceptance of the union.

At the thought of his family's wholehearted support, another swirl of regret swept through him. He told himself it didn't matter, that he'd make the best of the short-term marriage and that his family would never know the difference.

His gaze returned to Sawyer Fortune, who sat next to Asher. His barroom buddy sported a playful grin that said, "Better you than me, dude."

If he only knew.

But then again, romance and promises of forever aside, Miguel was about to marry the woman he'd once loved more than life itself. The woman whose desperate plea and financial offer was making it possible for him to open his nightclub within the next month or two.

The woman who'd…

Oh, wow. The woman who'd just entered the courtyard, looking like a lovely dream come true.

The maid of honor, Marnie McCafferty, led the way,

but Miguel couldn't take his eyes off his dazzling bride. That dress had looked great when she'd tried it on for him last Saturday night. But today? With her hair swept up in a pile of curls, a sizable pair of diamond studs in her ears…?

Damn. If he weren't careful, he just might fall head-over-heels in love with her all over again. And that—more than sex—would complicate things for him.

As music sounded and Marnie started down the short aisle, Miguel watched Nicole, struck by her beauty, by the way she bit down on her bottom lip as though she were a pauper in princess clothing.

They'd nearly pulled it off. Just a few more steps.

He caught her gaze and cast her a charming smile. *We can do it, honey.*

The silent communication seemed to lighten her load, to lift her mood.

Before he knew it, she was at his side, and for the next few minutes, Miguel forgot the whole wedding was a sham.

As the justice of the peace spoke, Nicole tried her best to listen, to focus on the vows she was about to make. Yet she couldn't help stealing a glance at her parents, who sat in the front row.

She'd broken down this morning and had decided to call them, even before Miguel had suggested she do so. And she'd told them she was getting married today. She'd invited them to attend—if they could hide their disappointment and try to be supportive.

They'd complained about the short notice, about the hasty mistake she was about to make, but they'd asked where they were supposed to be and when.

Her father hadn't mentioned anything about walking her down the aisle or giving her away—and she hadn't brought it up. After that last stunt he'd pulled, she'd decided to skip that "special" part of the wedding. As a result, she'd moved down the aisle with a newfound sense of freedom—as well as a tinge of regret.

And now that her marriage plan was all coming into play, her heart scrambled to make sense of it all, especially the whacky, unexpected feeling she had for Miguel.

She wouldn't call it love, though. She couldn't call it that. But just being with him today, sensing his friendship, set off an unexpected boost of confidence, of peace, of strength.

"Do you take this man," the justice of the peace began.

Nicole couldn't help but look at Miguel with a yearning based upon… What? The love they were about to claim was real?

He'd suggested they write their own vows, which might have been nice had the circumstances been different. But she'd refused to consider it for fear it would make her think too hard about what she might actually feel for him.

When the justice of the peace asked the standard questions, she answered, "I do."

Next it was Miguel's turn.

When he said, "I do," his voice clear and decisive, she could almost believe he meant those words from the bottom of his heart.

"By the power vested in me by the state of Texas," the justice of the peace said, "I now pronounce you husband and wife."

With that, Miguel took her in his arms and kissed her—sweet and tender and all too brief for a man whose vow of love had been real.

So what more had she expected? And why had she found it so darn disappointing?

"Ladies and gentlemen," the smiling officiate announced, "may I be the first to introduce Mr. and Mrs. Miguel Mendoza."

The wedding guests broke out in cheers and applause, while Nicole's parents merely sat there, her dad's expression unreadable, her mom wearing a wistful smile, her eyes red-rimmed and watery.

As if sensing her discomfort, Miguel took her by the hand, giving her fingers a warm and gentle squeeze, reminding her that she had someone in her corner, even if that sweet someone had been bought and paid for.

"Nicole and I are glad that you came to share our special day with us," Miguel told their guests. "We'd also like to thank J.R. and Isabella for allowing us to have the ceremony at Molly's Pride."

"It was our pleasure," J.R. said, taking a stand and extending his arm toward an arched doorway. "Please join us for drinks and refreshments on the patio."

At that point, Nicole's father got to his feet, and her

mother followed suit. As the older couple approached Miguel and Nicole, her father's expression finally softened.

He kissed Nicole's cheek. "You look beautiful, baby girl. I only regret that you didn't give us time to get used to all of this—and to give us an opportunity to provide the kind of wedding your mother had always wanted you to have."

Nicole's mom sniffled and wiped her eyes with a damp, twisted handkerchief. "You're a beautiful bride, sweetheart. But then, I always knew you would be."

At that heartfelt truth, Nicole felt a dual stab of guilt and regret. Her eyes filled with tears. She wished things would have been different, that her mother could have helped her plan the perfect wedding—to the perfect groom, of course.

"You didn't even have a photographer," her mother added.

"My brother will take a few shots during the reception," Miguel said. "And we'll pose with the justice of the peace before he leaves."

Her father reached into the pocket of his lapel, pulled out an envelope and handed it to Miguel. "We didn't have time to get a card, but here you go, son. Use it wisely."

Miguel tensed momentarily, then accepted what had to be a gift of cash. "Thank you. Nicole will use it to decorate the new house."

She suspected he wanted her parents to know that he wouldn't spend the money on himself, although they had no idea that the house would remain in her name alone and that he'd pack up and leave one day, taking only the clothes he'd brought with him.

"When do you plan to move in?" her mother asked.

"As soon as we return from our honeymoon." Miguel slid his arm around Nicole and drew her close, making them two against the world.

The warmth of his touch, the strength of his grip, set her heart soaring. For a moment, it all seemed real. Maybe not the vows they'd made moments ago, but the team they'd just formed.

Too bad they hadn't been able to make a stand like this when they'd been young and in love.

"Where are you going on your honeymoon?" her mother asked.

"Miguel is surprising me. I have no idea, although he told me to pack a passport, a swimsuit and clothing suitable for warm weather."

"If you'll excuse us," her father said, cutting the conversation short and nodding toward the arched doorway that led to the Fortunes' patio. "Your mom and I need to go. We had other plans today and had to postpone them to fit this in."

She hadn't needed the reminder. He'd said as much this morning when she'd called to invite them.

"I'm sorry for the short notice," Nicole said again, even though they all knew she could have mentioned an actual day and time at least a week ago.

"Come on," her dad said to her mom. "We're running late as it is, and we need to thank the Fortunes for hosting the ceremony."

And with that, her parents were off. And just as swiftly, so was the pressure that had been building ever since their arrival at Molly's Pride.

Before Nicole and Miguel left the now empty courtyard, he asked, "How are you holding up?"

"I'm fine. How about you? My dad can be so…"

"Patronizing?" Miguel chuffed. "Tell me about it. The wedding is over, and we're married. All we need to do is sign the license. He'll just have to get used to it—and to me."

She could have reminded him that this was a marriage of convenience. And that, in spite of what the justice of the peace had proclaimed just moments ago, they wouldn't stay together until death parted them.

"Besides," Miguel said, "we have a plane to catch."

"I'm surprised that, with everything you've got going on with the building, you're still planning to take a week off."

"Your parents might be leaving now, but you can be sure that they'll be watching us closely over the next few months, and I don't want to give them any reason to doubt that our marriage isn't the real deal."

She could appreciate that. Miguel was also a man of his word. He'd made an agreement and would do everything he could to abide by it.

"So what time is our flight?" she asked.

"I told the pilot we'd be at the airport and ready to leave by three o'clock."

He'd spoken directly to the pilot? "We're not going on a commercial airline?"

"Do you know Tanner Redmond?" he asked.

"The name sounds familiar."

"Tanner's married to Jordana Fortune, Wendy's sister. He also owns a flight school and charter service. And I booked the trip with him."

Okay, so the "idea man" had clearly made some solid travel plans in advance, using family connections. The passport requirement suggested they'd be leaving the country, maybe flying to Mexico or the Caribbean. If that was the case, the swimsuits and summer clothing made sense.

"You're still not going to tell me where we're going?" she asked.

"Does it matter?"

"Not really."

"Good. Let's go to the patio and spend the required time with our guests, then we can get the trip under way. Sawyer said he'd drop us off at the airport."

So Miguel had everything under control.

Nicole had told him earlier that it didn't matter where they were going. After all, she hadn't given the honeymoon much thought since it was only a facade, just as the wedding ceremony had been.

But as they started toward the arched doorway that led to the patio, Miguel placed his hand on the small of her back, sending a spiral of heat to her core and triggering thoughts of romance and moonlit walks in the sand.

Moments ago, she'd thought it didn't matter where

they went. In fact, she wouldn't have minded if they'd just stayed at home in Red Rock.

But now, as Miguel slipped his arm around her waist, claiming her as his bride, the details of their trip seemed to matter a whole lot more than they had before. And she couldn't help wondering what her husband, the "idea man," had planned for the next seven days.

Sawyer, who couldn't fit them in the sporty Jaguar XK convertible he owned, drove Nicole and Miguel to Red Rock Regional Airport in Nicole's Lexus.

"I'll be back to pick you up on Friday afternoon," he told Miguel, when he dropped them and their luggage off at the curb. "You've got my number. Just give me a call if there's some reason you won't arrive on time."

Miguel thanked his friend, not just for the ride to the airport, but for setting up the flight. When Sawyer had learned that Miguel was going to take Nicole to the Yucatán Peninsula on a commercial airline, he'd suggested they use a charter service—as a wedding gift from him.

"It's too much," Miguel had said.

"No, it's not. I'll get the family rate. Besides, you can return the favor by covering my tab on opening night at Mendoza's."

"You got a deal," Miguel had said.

Now, as Sawyer pulled away from the curb, Miguel escorted Nicole into the waiting area just off the lobby of the two-story terminal. "Laurel Redmond said she'd meet us there," said Miguel.

"I thought the pilot's name was Tanner."

"Tanner owns the charter service as well as a flight school and had planned to take us. But he called me earlier this morning, saying there'd been a slight change in plans. His sister will be our pilot today. But I'm sure she's just as competent. She racked up her flying experience while she was in the Air Force."

"Impressive," Nicole said.

He thought so, too.

Ten minutes later, they were met by an attractive, blue-eyed blonde, her hair pulled back in a ponytail, her demeanor all business.

"Mr. Mendoza?" she asked. "I'm Laurel Redmond."

He reached out his hand in greeting. "Please, call me Miguel. And this is my wife, Nicole."

It felt a little surreal to be claiming her as his wife, yet that's what she was now. At least, for the time being.

"It's a good day for a flight," Laurel said. "The weather should be nice all the way."

"I'm glad to hear it." Miguel reached for his suitcase.

"Then let's go." Laurel led the way out of the terminal and to the plane, a Beechcraft King Air 350.

When they reached the open door with a built-in stairway that enabled them to board, Nicole turned to Miguel. "Are you still keeping our destination a surprise?"

He chuckled. "No, not anymore. We're going to Suenos del Sol, a beachfront resort on the Yucatán Peninsula."

"Your uncle's place?" she asked.

For a moment he questioned his choice, realizing she

might not feel the same way he did about his favorite vacation spot.

"It's certainly not a five-star hotel," he said, "but I think you'll like it."

"I'm sure I will." She flashed him a pretty smile that validated her words. "You used to talk about it all the time when we were in high school, about how your family used to stay there sometimes. And I thought it sounded like a cool place."

Back then, when they'd been teenagers in love and he'd actually believed they stood a chance of having a real marriage, he'd thought the resort would make a great honeymoon spot. Maybe that's why he'd thought about it now, when a romantic getaway had come in handy.

He had to admit that he'd been waiting for days— hell, maybe even years—to whisk Nicole away from her parents and to have her to himself in a tropical paradise, to see if their chemistry was still as hot as it once was.

And he had every reason to believe that they would set the nights on fire. After all, he'd be in his element at Suenos del Sol. And he wasn't just talking about knowing his way around the beachfront setting.

He'd wined and dined his share of women before, so he knew all the right words to say, all the right moves to make. But Nicole was more than just one of his past conquests, and he'd never been so determined to win a woman's heart....

No, not her heart.

Yet as he stole a glance her way, watched her settle

into her seat and buckle up for takeoff, he wondered just what it was that he was feeling for her.

And why it seemed so important to plan a romantic trip with her, complete with all the props.

Somewhere in the back of the plane, two crystal flutes, a bottle of champagne on ice and long-stemmed, chocolate-covered strawberries they would enjoy during the flight had been packed and prepared.

Another surprise Miguel had wanted to spring.

As he adjusted his own seat belt, he thought about what he'd lined up for the next week and smiled, pleased with himself.

When he'd first brought up the idea of a romantic getaway, Nicole had been clearly taken aback. *You're planning a* honeymoon?

Yes, ma'am. The best one ever.

He'd explained that they shouldn't give her parents any reason to suspect that she'd countered their legal maneuvering with one of her own. He'd also told her that he intended their marriage, as short as it might be, to be real in every sense of the word.

And how much more real could it get than a week spent on a secluded stretch of tropical beach—swimsuits optional?

It's not right, his brother Marcos had said when Miguel admitted what he and Nicole had planned to do.

Miguel had shared his rationale for doing so with his brother, which he considered sound. Yet now, for the first time since agreeing to marry Nicole, Miguel began to question his motives.

Not just for agreeing to be a husband for hire, which had made sense for practical reasons, but his determination to sweep her off her feet while they were at Suenos del Sol, to remind her of what they'd once had—and how good it had been.

Sure, there were definitely sex-based reasons for pulling out all the romantic stops. He was only human—and so was she.

But was there more to his efforts than just wanting to make love? More than a natural desire to satisfy the raging physical needs?

Did he, at least on some level, hope to stir up those old feelings she'd once had for him?

It was possible, he supposed. And if that was indeed a subconscious part of his plan, his brother's words came back to haunt him.

It's not right, man.

And Miguel had to admit that it wasn't. Why should he try to stir up Nicole's emotions and memories when he was hell-bent not to let that happen to him?

When he finally walked away from her with a divorce in hand and the money she'd promised him invested in his nightclub, the last thing he wanted to take with him was regret or even the whisper of a broken heart.

So why work so hard at sweeping her off her feet and set her up for that same risk? Did he want her to experience some of the pain he'd felt when they'd broken up all those years ago?

No, it wasn't that.

At least, not completely.

But could it be a small part?

As the plane sped down the runway and began to lift off, Miguel glanced out the window, watching the Texas countryside fade into the distance.

So what was he really trying to do?

Relive a sweet memory?

Or extract a bit of revenge?

As much as he hated to admit it, maybe a little bit of both. And if that was the case, what kind of man did that make him?

Chapter Nine

Nearly four hours later, after Miguel and Nicole shared champagne and strawberries on their flight over the Gulf of Mexico, the plane touched down at Santa Inez, an international airport located about five miles from the Suenos del Sol Resort on the Yucatan Peninsula.

The terminal, if you could call it that, was a single, three-sided building that opened in back for easy boarding of passengers and luggage. Unless things had changed since the last time Miguel had been to visit *Tio* Pepe, there were only two international flights that flew in and out each day, both of which came from the United States.

"I'll be back to get you next week," Laurel said, as they stepped away from the plane. "If for some reason your schedule changes, you have my cell number, as well as Tanner's."

"By the way," Miguel told the pilot, "I know you have to wait for the plane to be refueled, so you might want to check out the taco stand on the front side of the building. I know some people are leery about eating anything from an outdoor vendor, but I'd highly recommend that you try one of Beto's. They're probably the best you'll ever eat."

Laurel smiled. "I've done a lot of traveling while in the Air Force, so I'm pretty adventurous when it comes to the food I eat. Thanks for the tip."

After they told Laurel goodbye and wished her a nice flight back to Red Rock, Miguel and Nicole walked inside toward the two Mexican customs officers who made a quick scan of their bags.

Once they were free to go and outside the building, Miguel asked, "How adventurous are *you* when it comes to trying food?"

She laughed. "I'm afraid that I filled up on champagne and those awesome chocolate-covered strawberries. So I'd better pass on the tacos."

"Suit yourself." He nodded toward the vehicle his uncle routinely sent to pick up the hotel guests who'd flown in to stay at Suenos del Sol. "Come on, there's our ride."

They headed toward the old turquoise woodie wagon that sat idling on the side of the road, a flamingo-pink surfboard attached to the roof, the tailgate lifted.

Ramon Torres, the heavyset, middle-aged driver,

stood beside the open passenger door, wearing a pair of huaraches, khaki slacks and a blue-and-yellow Hawaiian shirt.

"We're going to ride in that old woodie?" she asked. "How cool is that?"

He laughed. "I'd love to buy that one from my uncle and take it back to Red Rock."

"You have to be kidding. What would you do with it?"

"A 1949 Ford woodie wagon? I'd refurbish it."

"And then sell it? I'll bet some wealthy surfer in Southern California would love to have one."

"Maybe so, but I'd probably keep it for myself."

Ramon, who'd worked for *Tio* Pepe for nearly thirty years, grinned broadly as they reached the car.

"Miguel!" His brown eyes lit up, and his mustachioed smile broadened. "It's good to finally see you again. This must be your beautiful bride."

She was beautiful all right, even though she'd left the wedding dress back at Molly's Pride and donned a pair of white jeans and a turquoise-colored blouse for the flight to Mexico.

Miguel, who'd shed his Armani suit in favor of shorts and a Tommy Bahama shirt, greeted Ramon with a robust hug. Then he introduced his wife, adding, "She *is* lovely, isn't she? I'm one lucky guy, Ramon. I just had to bring her down here and show her off."

"*Mucho* gusto," Ramon said. Then he took their luggage from them and placed both bags in back.

After lowering the tailgate, Ramon waited outside the vehicle until Miguel and Nicole slid into the backseat.

Moments later, they were off, the old woodie chugging and bumping and swerving along the dusty, pot-holed road that led to the resort.

Normally on the ride to Suenos del Sol, Miguel looked forward to the wide turn in the road and passing the lookout point the locals called Punta Vista.

He would usually crane his neck, trying to catch his first glimpse of the aquamarine water and the white sandy stretch of beach.

But today he was more interested in watching Nicole and waiting for her reaction at seeing the amazing view for the very first time.

She, like him, hadn't talked much on the flight from Red Rock, so he wasn't sure what she was thinking, what she was feeling. Was her father the only one who regretted their marriage?

As the woodie bumped along a dusty dirt road, Nicole glanced out the open window at the Mexican countryside. The flight to the Yucatán Peninsula had been as smooth as Laurel had told them they could expect.

It had also been quiet, mostly because Miguel had been so silent and preoccupied after takeoff.

During the first hour or so, Nicole had been lost in her thoughts, too. She'd been wondering what Miguel had planned for their honeymoon, intrigued by the possibilities, yet uneasy by them, as well. She especially struggled with the sleeping arrangement, since she doubted he'd reserved a two-bedroom suite.

But after the flight was well under way, Miguel had remained pensive. She'd first thought he might be thinking about how much he missed his favorite vacation spot or about the uncle he hadn't seen in a while. But when the silence continued, she'd begun to worry that something more serious might be weighing on his mind.

About the time they were halfway through the flight, Laurel had reminded him he had champagne chilling in the back of the plane. And at that point, he'd seemed to perk up and shake off his thoughtful mood.

Yet now that they were in the woodie and headed for the resort, he seemed to have slipped back into that tall, dark and brooding mode again.

"How much farther is the hotel?" she asked.

"We're getting pretty close now." He pointed up ahead, where a group of palm trees grew. "In fact, you'll be able to see the ocean soon, as well as the *palapa*-style roofs of the hotel once we make the next turn."

As the woodie swung around the curve in the road, revealing Nicole's first glimpse of the turquoise waters of the Caribbean, she couldn't help but comment about the beauty. "Would you look at the color of the ocean?"

"There's nothing like the view—or the location," Miguel said. "But like I told you before, the resort itself isn't quite what you're used to in terms of accommodations, but it's clean and comfortable."

She reached across the seat and placed her hand on

his arm. "I'm not as stuck-up as you think. I'm sure it'll be just fine."

The intensity in his gaze locked on hers and darn near squeezed the breath right out of her. And for one soul-stirring moment, she wondered if his earlier silence had something to do with old feelings coming back to haunt him and the realization that they'd be spending a week together in a tropical, beachfront paradise.

The possibility sent her senses reeling and her heart racing. Rather than deal with the possibility that she might be right, she turned away, breaking the connection, and again studied the amazing view.

Yet it was the man who sat beside her she found more intriguing than her surroundings. Because if truth be told, she wasn't sure those old feelings hadn't come back to haunt her, as well.

"Here we are," Ramon, the driver, announced, as he pulled to a stop in front of an open-air lobby which boasted a tropical decor that reminded her a bit of Old Hawaii.

Miguel climbed from the car, then waited for Nicole to exit. Once she did, she scanned the hotel grounds, noting a setting sun, palm trees swaying in the breeze, lush hanging plants and vines. The newly mown lawn stretched all the way to the white sand beach.

Miguel had been right, the hotel itself wasn't fancy. But the setting was amazing.

Once they entered the lobby, a tall, silver-haired man in shorts and a Hawaiian-style shirt greeted Miguel with a hug.

"Nicole," Miguel said, "this is *Tio* Pepe, my uncle."

The older man turned to her with a smile. "I'm so happy to welcome you—not only to Suenos del Sol, but to the Mendoza family."

"After I check in," Miguel began, "I'll…"

"It's all taken care of." Pepe nodded to a young man who was clearly a bellman. "Take them to Bungalow Twelve in the honeymoon wing."

The bellman nodded, then reached for their bags and put them on the wheeled cart.

"Thank you," Miguel told his uncle. "As soon as we're settled, we'll be down. I'd like to buy you a drink."

"I'd like that," Pepe said. "It will give me an opportunity to chat with your new wife, to get to know her."

"I'm looking forward to it," Nicole said. "Miguel has spoken so highly of you that I'm glad we finally have a chance to meet in person."

Pepe offered her the warmest of smiles. "And I've heard a lot about you, too." Then he turned to the bellman. "Take them to their room and make sure they have everything they need."

The young man nodded, then ushered them down a walkway, around a swimming pool and past an outdoor bar, where several couples sipped piña coladas and mai tais. Then he took them to one of several cottages which stood on stilts and were covered with *palapa* roofs.

He used a key to open the door to a quaint but clean cottage on the beach. It had hardwood flooring, an overstuffed sofa with a blue tropical print and a glass-top coffee table.

* * *

While the bellman pointed out the coffeepot and told Miguel where he could find the ice machine, Nicole decided to explore their accommodations and made her way to the arched doorway of the bedroom which had a sliding door that opened onto the deck.

In the center of the room was a queen-size bed festooned with a gauzy white canopy.

A single bed, she realized. But then again, that shouldn't surprise her since Pepe had instructed the bellman to take them to the honeymoon wing.

Well, so much for thinking they could figure out some kind of reasonable sleeping arrangements.

As soon as Miguel tipped the bellman and they were alone, Nicole turned to her new husband and crossed her arms. "This is going to be awkward."

"Don't worry, your virtue is safe." He pointed to the sofa. "I'll take the couch."

A pang of disappointment shot right through her, even though she should have been relieved that he'd come up with a workable solution.

"Do you want to use the bathroom first?" he asked.

Sure. Why not?

She opened her suitcase and removed the pale blue sundress she'd packed. Then she padded into the bathroom and freshened up from their flight.

When she was finished, and Miguel had gone in to take his turn, she went to the bedroom and unpacked her suitcase. Then she opened the sliding door of their beachfront bungalow and stepped onto the raised deck that looked over the teal-blue water that stretched across the horizon as far as the eye could see.

The sun had dropped low in the west, painting the sky in streaks of lavender, pink and orange, promising a beautiful sunset.

Nicole stood at the railing for a moment, marveling at the ocean view, relishing the salty scent of a balmy tropical breeze, lulled by the sound of the waves breaking on the shore.

Miguel had been right. Suenos del Sol might not be the fanciest resort, but what an amazing setting. It was just the kind of place a driven, hard-working executive could get away from the corporate grind.

No matter what happened this week, she would use the time to rest and recoup from all the headaches she'd had to deal with for as long as she'd been the vice president of Castleton Boots.

Funny how she hadn't realized how badly she'd needed a break until she got here, until she saw how therapeutic a few lazy days could be.

Miguel's family used to vacation at Suenos del Sol, but so far, she hadn't seen many families with kids—mostly couples, like the older man and woman who were now walking hand in hand along a stretch of lawn near the pool or the two people reading books while seated on towels stretched across the sand.

Obviously, Suenos del Sol was a romantic getaway that catered to newlyweds and couples. Or maybe it just seemed that way because Pepe had assigned them to one of the honeymoon cottages.

"Are you ready to go?" Miguel asked from the doorway of the bedroom.

Nicole turned from her spot on the deck and smiled. "Yes. I was just taking in the view."

"Me, too." His gaze, which was clearly on her rather than the ocean or resort grounds, sketched over her, just as a light wind kicked up, billowing the gauzy material of her sundress.

An amazing rush shot through her, and not just from the tropical breeze that blew wisps of her hair across her face and whispered against her skin.

Something in Miguel's expression—the intensity, the passion that darkened his eyes—sent an arrow of heat straight to her belly.

She expected him to make a move at that point, to cross the room, take her in his arms and tell her again how he intended to make their marriage real in every sense of the word.

Yet he merely stood there, leaning against the doorjamb. Undressing her with his eyes, seducing her without saying a word.

Something told her that if they were going to come together, she'd have to take the first step toward him, toward the bed. But she wouldn't do that. She *couldn't*.

Sex would only complicate their business arrangement. But tell that to her soaring heart and her raging hormones.

This—sharing a hotel room, but not a bed—was *so* not going to work. Being near Miguel and not being able to touch him was going to kill her.

And if that wasn't bad enough, being surrounded by other vacationing couples—newly married and those enjoying a second honeymoon—would only make it worse.

He might have volunteered to sleep on the sofa, but that wasn't going to be a very good solution. Not when something sexual seemed to be unfolding right before her very eyes, tempting her beyond measure—and against her better judgment.

Six nights.

Two ex-lovers.

One bed.

It all added up to trouble in paradise.

What had she been thinking when she'd flown to New York and proposed a rushed marriage to a man she'd once loved?

Doing her best to shake off the attraction and to break the spell Miguel had cast on her just a couple heartbeats ago, Nicole cleared her throat. "We'd better go. We don't want to keep your uncle waiting."

"All right. Let's get out of here."

That sounded simple enough. And while she'd been the one to suggest they leave, the truth of the matter was that she wouldn't mind ordering room service and remaining right where they were.

Yet even if *Tio* Pepe wasn't waiting for them in the lounge, she wouldn't suggest making love here and now. Not when nothing good could possibly come of it.

Yet her whole body was reminding her just how long it had been since they'd had a good workout.

Oh, for Pete's sake. How in the world was she ever going to get through the next week without falling prey to temptation?

Miguel and Nicole spent the first evening of their honeymoon with *Tio* Pepe in the Suenos del Sol lounge.

If his uncle thought it was unusual for a new bride and groom to enjoy time in his company, rather than in the privacy of their room, he didn't comment.

Either way, having Pepe with them made it a lot easier for Miguel to ignore the jolt of sexual awareness that had nearly blown off the thatched *palapa* roof of the bungalow the moment he had peered into the bedroom and saw a dreamy-eyed Nicole standing on the deck, the only thing between them an empty bed.

Miguel hadn't acted on it, even though he'd planned a romantic getaway, hoping to make love for old times' sake. And while he'd like nothing more than to have a sexual romp with Nicole, it would have to be her idea because he couldn't trust himself to make love to her for all the right reasons—and none of the wrong ones.

Only trouble was, his attraction to her had ignited all over again, threatening to take him down in a blaze of glory.

This is going to be awkward, she'd told him upon their arrival in the bungalow. But it would entail a hell of a lot worse than stilted conversations.

When he'd spotted her standing out on the deck, her cheeks flushed, her eyes bright, the breeze playing with wisps of her hair and the flimsy fabric of her dress, he'd completely forgotten that they weren't on a real honey-moon and that she wasn't really his wife.

At that moment, he wished he could roll back the clock to the time when he hadn't given any thought to his motives for wanting to make love with her again, other than a little mutual pleasure.

"This is amazing," Nicole said, as she munched on a homemade tortilla chip dipped in seviche. The fresh fish and shrimp had been marinated in lemon juice and spiced with chili peppers, *Tio* Pepe's personal recipe. "I've seen this on various menus but I've never tried it before."

Miguel lifted his ice-cold bottle of Pacifico beer and took a drink, trying his best to focus on his uncle and not the beautiful brunette who sat beside him, nursing a glass of ice water laced with a slice of lemon.

"So tell me," he said to Pepe, "is Las Palmas still a hot nightspot for the tourists?"

"Yes, it is. At least, for those who like to kick up their heels and have a good time. Our honeymooners tend to want to stick close to the bungalows—and take midnight swims. Know what I mean?"

Miguel knew exactly what he meant. And under nor-mal circumstances, he'd much rather stick close to the bungalow with Nicole, only leaving the bedroom long enough to eat or to cool off in the ocean.

"You told me about that nightclub years ago," Nicole said. "Isn't that the one that sparked your dream to open a club of your own someday?"

Miguel smiled, glad she remembered. "My parents

used to bring us down here for vacations and even once for a family reunion. When Marcos and I were teenagers and supposed to be asleep in our room, we'd slip away and sneak into Las Palmas. We loved listening to the music and watching the people dance."

"The last time I talked to your father," Pepe said, "he mentioned that you were going to open your own club in Red Rock this summer."

Miguel nodded, chest puffing up more than a smidgeon and a big ol' grin stretching across his face. "I'm going to call it Mendoza's. You'll have to come see it."

Pepe lifted his beer and took a swig. "I'd like that, *mijo.* Will it be like Las Palmas, with the tropical decor and disco music?"

"No, I don't think that would go over very well in Red Rock. Mendoza's is going to cater to the country-western crowd."

When the cocktail waitress stopped by their table and asked if they'd like another drink, Miguel suggested dinner.

"I'm ready to eat," Nicole said. "How about you, *Tio* Pepe? Can you join us?"

Miguel's uncle slowly shook his head. "As much as I'd like to, I have a beautiful lady of my own, fixing dinner for me at her place."

Pepe's wife had died of cancer about five years ago, and while most of the single women in town between the ages of thirty-five and sixty had been only too happy to take her place in his heart, he'd held off on dating.

"Have I met her?" Miguel asked.

"No, but I'll probably introduce you to her before you and Nicole have to leave."

"I'll look forward to it, Tio."

Pepe nodded as he slid back his chair and stood. He reached for Nicole's hand and gave it a warm shake with both of his. "I wish only the best for you two. I'll see you in the morning. Have a wonderful evening."

Miguel didn't know about that. He kind of liked having a third wheel to diffuse the sexual tension, but he cast his uncle a grin, then reached for Nicole's hand. "Come on, honey. Suenos del Sol has one of the best chefs on the peninsula. Wait until you taste the mahimahi."

A couple of hours later, after a scrumptious dinner at a cozy table for two, Miguel led Nicole back to the bungalow, their path lit by tiki lights.

"It's a pretty night," she said. "Look at the moon and stars."

He already had, when they'd first left the restaurant and started along the path to the bungalow. The evening sky had been made for lovers.

"I can see why this resort would be your favorite vacation spot," she added—making small talk, he supposed.

He couldn't blame her for that. The night lay before them, the romantic possibilities endless. He could slip his hand in hers again, like he'd done when they'd left the lounge and gone into the restaurant. But he didn't.

When they reached bungalow number twelve, he reached into his pocket and pulled out the key to their room, using it to open the door. Then he turned on the light.

Now what? he wondered, as he scanned the living area and realized there wasn't a television in sight.

"I think I'll turn in for the night," Nicole said. "I'm tired. It's been a long day."

"Me, too," he lied. "Why don't you go ahead and use the bathroom first. I'll make up a bed on the sofa."

"We can trade off," she said. "I'll let you have the bed tomorrow."

"That's not necessary."

She could have objected, but she didn't. So while she gathered her toiletry bag from the bureau, along with a nightgown she'd placed in the drawer, he joined her in the bedroom, where he opened the closet and removed the extra blanket and pillow from the shelf, then went to make up the couch.

All the while, she watched him through the open bedroom door. Again, she could have said something, stopped him, but didn't.

Instead, she padded into the bathroom, closing the door.

Damn. He'd been sure she was going to say something, suggest something. But she hadn't.

And since he was determined to let her make the first move when it came to sex, he realized it was going to be a long night—and a hell of a long week.

Chapter Ten

Miguel slept like hell that first night and not much better on the five that followed. In spite of the sofa having fairly soft cushions, he never seemed to be able to find a comfortable spot.

By the time each morning rolled around, his back ached and he usually had a crick in his neck.

Several times, while opening up a bottle of ibuprofen, he'd been tempted to ask the front desk to give him a separate room, the news of which was sure to reach his uncle's ears and blow the whole wedding ruse sky-high. So instead, he'd sucked it up and made the best of it.

He kept hoping Nicole would ask him to join her in the bed, and he would have jumped at the chance for more reasons than a good night's rest. But so far, she hadn't. And with one last day in paradise, sleeping curled up beside her didn't look promising.

He could have turned on the charm until the suggestion to make love came from her lips, but he refused to seduce her on principle alone. If she made the first move toward sex, he wouldn't have to question his motives—or the kind of man he really was.

So now he knew. He'd passed his own test.

But just barely.

Things might be platonic between them, but on the upside, they seemed to be getting to know each other all over again. Still the sexual tension stretched between them like a strained and frayed rubber band, ready to snap at any given time.

The brutal sleep regimen, along with the self-imposed celibacy, was doing a real number on him. And with his hormones on overload, he just might pop himself. But he could finally count down the hours until life went back to normal—or as normal as a marriage for business purposes could get.

As dawn broke over Suenos del Sol on their last day at the resort, the morning unfolded much like the others had.

Nicole had come out of the bedroom all bright-eyed and bushy tailed, as if she'd slept like a charm. Then Miguel had padded into the bathroom, hoping a hot shower would ease his aches and pains.

For the most part, it had.

They'd had coffee in their room, while deciding how they'd spend the day. During the week, they'd found a nearby stable and gone horseback riding. They'd also taken a Jeep tour of the area. Miguel had even put some of his charm to good use by talking Nicole into parasailing.

Not that they hadn't spent a few lazy hours reading by the pool, although Nicole had to set her book aside several times to either make a call to her office to Diana or to receive one from her executive assistant—some guy named Bradley.

"So what'll it be today?" Miguel asked her. "We could borrow a car from my uncle and drive to Cancún."

"I suppose we could, but I spotted a poster in the lobby yesterday that advertised an art show and a farmer's market in Santa Inez. Why don't we rent bicycles and go check it out?"

The idea was as good as any he could come up with, so he said, "Sure. Why not?"

After a light breakfast, they rented two beach cruisers and rode into town to a large grassy area with outdoor booths where vendors sold produce and handmade items, such as tie-dye shirts, ceramics and other work created by local artisans.

They made their way past the food selections, where one woman displayed a variety of homemade sweet breads and rolls and another offered fresh salsa bottled in mason jars. They spotted several booths of handcrafted jewelry, as well as one that offered wind chimes made out of colorful melted glass and bamboo.

They stopped at a table stacked high with quilts, then moved on to one with crocheted baby blankets.

Eventually, they made their way to the spot where several artists displayed ceramic sculptures, paintings, watercolors and charcoal sketches.

"Look," Nicole said, pointing to an oil painting perched on an easel. "What do you think?"

It was the view at Punta Vista at sunset, the *palapa* rooftops of Suenos del Sol showing in the distance.

"I like the colors," he said. "It's a nice reminder of our…trip." He nearly said "honeymoon," although it had been anything but. Still, he had gotten a chance to know the adult Nicole better.

And he had to admit that he liked her, especially when she wasn't carrying her smartphone with her.

"This really doesn't fit with the decor of my condo," she said. "But I can find a place for it in the new house."

"How much?" Miguel asked the artist.

"*No habla Ingles,* senor." The man scanned the grounds, as if looking for an interpreter.

"*Esta bien,*" Miguel told him, lapsing into Spanish.

While they negotiated a price, Nicole's cell phone rang.

So what else was new? She might be on vacation, but her mind was back in Red Rock, at the Castleton Boots office.

"Yes, Bradley. That's exactly what needs to happen. Can you handle that today? It can't wait until I get back to the office on Monday morning."

It hadn't taken Miguel long to realize her father might have been right about one thing. Nicole seemed to be married to her work. Was that why she'd had to come to New York, asking him to be her phony husband?

It seemed hard to believe that she wasn't dating anyone seriously. She'd also told him that Castleton Boots was her life.

Of course, Nicole had always been responsible and driven. Just look at the kind of student she was in high school. Maybe she'd just turned that drive into the family business.

It was hard to say for sure, though. While she still had some of the same traits, she wasn't the same person she'd been ten years ago.

Of course, neither was he.

In some ways, he supposed, it was nice to have this time away—and a chance to get to know each other all over again.

When she ended the call, Miguel shot her a grin. "Congratulations. You've just purchased a painting sure to brighten up that new house."

She returned his smile, her eyes lighting up, reminding him of the girl she'd once been, the fun-loving, adventurous young woman he'd once loved. "Now we just have to figure out how to get it back to the hotel."

"That's all taken care of."

She cocked her head slightly. "What do you mean?"

He nodded toward the smiling artist. "Carlos here is going to have it delivered to the hotel for us."

"You think of everything."

Well, not everything. Their time in paradise was running out. And if he couldn't tempt her into suggesting a romantic adventure when she was a thousand miles from Red Rock—and her corporate office—how was he going to do it once they got home?

As Nicole lay stretched out on a woven beach mat, her body covered in sunblock, a seagull swooped across the late afternoon sky, followed by several more of the big white birds.

She and Miguel had returned to Suenos del Sol after shopping in town, then donned swimsuits and headed to the beach, deciding to spend some time in the sun.

Beside her, Miguel, who'd been seated in the sand and staring off into the water, got to his feet.

"I'm ready for a mai tai," he said. "How about you?"

"Sounds like a great idea."

Several minutes later, he returned with two of the tropical drinks in large souvenir glasses. "I figured you could always use another memory of our trip."

She sat up and took the pineapple-shaped glass from him. "Thanks."

Their so-called honeymoon was drawing to an end, and while it had been a little awkward at first—and still was, at times—she could say in all honesty that she'd enjoyed the time they'd spent together.

Over the last few days, they'd finally begun to relax a little in each other's presence. And now, as they sipped on their mai tais, they watched the horizon, where the colors of sunset had begun to stretch across the western sky.

A couple seagulls landed in the sand just a few feet

from their mats, cawing and fighting over a piece of seaweed.

Down the way, another couple lay on the sand, kissing, caressing and completely oblivious to the fact that they had an audience of two.

"Remember when it used to be like that for us?" he asked, taking his seat on the mat beside her. "When sex was new, and we couldn't keep our hands off each other?"

She remembered. "It wasn't just experimentation on my part. I was so caught up in…"

"What?"

She didn't answer. He knew what she meant. They'd been in love, and nothing else had mattered except being together, holding each other close, sharing their hopes and dreams, making promises….

None of which came true.

"Either way," he said, taking a seat beside her again, "I'll bet things would be better between us now. It's amazing what a little experience would add."

Speak for yourself, she was tempted to say. But she didn't want to let him know that she hadn't gotten that involved with anyone after him, especially when he'd…

Well, she had reason to believe he'd had plenty of conquests over the years. Besides, just look at him in those swim trunks.

She cast a glance at his body, nearly as naked as the day he was born, with that dark hair fluttering in the sea breeze, that olive coloring that made him appear tan, even in the dead of winter. Those broad shoulders, those taut abs…

And just a short reach away.

She took a sip of the mai tai, then pulled a long swallow, hoping to quench not only her thirst, but the heat pooled low in her belly, raging out of control in her veins.

Jeez. How had she managed to go this long without jumping his bones?

Because he'd been the perfect gentleman, she supposed.

"So why haven't you settled down?" he asked. "There must have been quite a few guys who've interested you over the years, men who…turned you inside out."

The only guy who'd been able to make her body yearn, to make it sing, had been Miguel. But she'd be darned if she'd let him know that he'd been her one and only.

After all, according to the Red Rock rumor mill, he was the ultimate bachelor who enjoyed traveling the country as a sales rep for a record company and who had a different woman every night.

He'd probably had hundreds of them. Thousands. And she'd only had…

Him.

She'd come close to having sex with someone else, a premed student she'd met in college. But she'd gotten cold feet somewhere between wet, slurpy kisses on the sofa and an "Oh, baby."

It had been lights-out-party's-over at that point.

Over the years, she'd questioned herself about that. Not her decision to refrain from going all the way with Steven, who'd already moved on to someone else the following weekend. But she'd wondered why she always seemed to back off from a relationship before anyone got too close.

Marnie had once suggested, since Miguel had been her first love and because of the promises they'd made each other, that Nicole somehow felt married to him in her heart. And that being with another guy would be cheating on him.

There could be something to that, Nicole supposed. But it was just as likely that the one she'd really be cheating was herself. After all, how disappointing would it be to learn that no one else would ever make her feel the way Miguel had when they'd been young lovers, stretched out in the backseat of his brother's car?

But enough of that, she told herself.

She took another drink of her mai tai before her musing turned into a mental blur of psychobabble. Then she sipped again and swallowed it down, feeling a warm buzz.

Unable to help herself, she stole another look at Miguel, who continued to watch the waves break on the sand.

A lock of hair had fallen across his brow, and without a conscious thought, she reached over and brushed it aside, just as if she still had every right to do so.

At her touch, he turned to face her. When their gazes met, something sparked deep inside her, igniting the heat that had been simmering under the surface since the day she'd seen Miguel at his office in New York.

Before she could give it a moment's thought, she leaned toward him, knowing instinctively he wouldn't move away. As their lips touched, she wrapped her arms around his neck, and the next thing she knew they were laying on the sand, necking as if they might never stop.

Their sunblock-scented bodies pressed together, their hands stroking, caressing, exploring.

Later she might blame her boldness on the tropical setting, on the rum in her drink, on the roar of the ocean urging something inside of her to rise up, to take what was rightfully hers. But for this one sweet moment, she wasn't going to think or analyze anything. She only wanted to feel what she'd been missing for the past ten years.

As if reading her mind, Miguel slid a hand along the curve of her back and down the bikini-clad slope of her hips, setting her memories soaring—while making a new one.

He pulled his lips from hers long enough to say, "There's a copse of trees just a few feet away. Let's take our towels over there. Or better yet, let's go back to the room, where we can be alone."

His fingers slid under the fabric string of her bathing suit, and a surge of desire shot right through her. She gave him one last kiss before moving, arching forward as she did, pressing her breasts against his chest, revealing her need, her desire.

As an "I love you" formed in her throat, she choked it back. No, she didn't love him. She couldn't. Not again.

Apprehension rose up inside. If they made love, she might fall for Miguel all over again—if she hadn't already. And then what?

He'd eventually go back to his bachelor life, just as she'd promised him he could do when the company was signed over to her. Only that life wouldn't be in New York, where she'd never have a chance to see him again, never risk running into him when he was out on a date, another woman on his arm.

Instead, he'd be in Red Rock, where she might run into him at any given time. And then where would that leave her?

Nicole placed her hands against his chest, pushing away from him, ending the kiss she'd just started.

"I can't do this."

"I know that. This is crazy. We don't need to make a scene out here. Let's go back to the room."

"No, I can't do it there, either."

His brow furrowed, and something shadowed the passion that had once glazed his eyes. "Why not?"

The question ricocheted inside her mind, begging for an answer and finding only one to use in place of what she really feared.

"We're planning a divorce," she said, struggling to catch her breath, "and it will be a lot easier if the marriage isn't consummated."

It was a lame excuse, she realized. But it was the

only one she could come up with when her mind had been scattered by lust.

"You have to be kidding." He sat upright.

She didn't dare try to explain herself. Not when her thoughts were a hodgepodge of old memories and new fears.

"I think it's time to go back into the room," she said, "but not to make love." She gathered up her towel, leaving him to get his own, then headed for the path that led to bungalow number twelve.

While they'd been necking on the beach like a couple of hormonal, love-struck teens, the sun had nearly dropped from sight, and the tiki lights came on to light her way.

When she entered the room, she went straight for the shower, washing all signs of sunblock, the sand and... Miguel from her body. But she doubted she'd ever be rid of his memory.

When she finally came out into the living area, he was seated on the sofa, staring at her as though she'd gone stark raving mad.

And maybe she had.

What crazy woman turned her back on the chance to have hot sex with Miguel Mendoza?

One who was smart enough to know when she'd get burned.

"I'm sorry," she said, as if that made it all better.

"Me, too." He stood, then nodded toward the bathroom. "I'm going to take a shower now."

She suspected it would be a cold one, and she was

sorry about that, as well. More sorry than she'd been when sending Steven home.

"You take the bed tonight," she told Miguel, as if that might somehow make things better. "I'll sleep on the sofa."

She wasn't sure, but she thought she'd heard him mutter a curse as he shut the bathroom door.

Either way, she pulled out the pillow, a sheet and a blanket, then she made her bed.

As she lay there in the fading twilight, as far from sleep as she'd ever been in her life, she thought about the last time she'd given a man reason to think that she wanted to make love, then changed her mind. There was an odd similarity.

She hadn't wanted to have sex with Steven because she had feared he'd never compare to Miguel.

And now?

Not only was she afraid of falling in love and losing him, she also feared that she'd never be able to compete with the sexually experienced women he'd dated.

The next morning, neither Miguel nor Nicole spoke of the night before. Instead, they moved about the bungalow, packing for the flight back to Red Rock. Once they checked out of the hotel, they told Miguel's uncle goodbye, thanking him for all he'd done to make sure their "honeymoon" was everything they'd hoped it would be and more. Then after warm embraces, they boarded the woodie wagon and rode back to the airport.

A couple times Nicole had opened her mouth to apologize or to explain, but she had stopped herself. After all, what was there to say?

She'd led him on, giving him every reason to believe that they would make love until dawn, then she'd backed out.

Did he think she was a tease? She certainly hadn't meant to be.

Once they arrived at Santa Inez International, Nicole expected to find Laurel Redmond waiting to fly them home. Instead, they were greeted by Laurel's brother, Tanner.

While they'd both been friendly with the pilot on the flight, Nicole wondered if it was obvious to Tanner that things were strained between the so-called newlyweds. If so, he didn't let on that he knew.

Instead of taking them directly back to Red Rock, Tanner landed the plane first in San Antonio, where Miguel and Nicole could go through U.S. customs. Then they made the short, up-and-down hop back to Red Rock.

They'd no more than climbed down the steps and started toward the terminal, their bags and Nicole's painting in hand, when they spotted a woman with a darling, chubby-cheeked baby boy riding on her hip.

"Looks like you have company," Miguel told Tanner.

When the pilot glanced at the window and spotted the woman, he broke into a big grin.

Nicole lowered her voice and asked Miguel, "Who is it?"

"That's Jordana, Wendy's sister and Tanner's wife.

The baby is their son, Jack. And the woman standing next to Jordana is Victoria Scarlett Fortune, Sawyer's sister. Well, you'd better scratch the Fortune. Victoria is married to Garrett Stone now."

As they entered the terminal, Jordana pointed at Tanner. "Look, Jack. There's Daddy."

The sweet little boy wriggled in his mother's arms, clearly thrilled to see his father, who greeted his wife with a kiss, then took the child in his arms.

Nicole had never been prone to fantasies about home and hearth, yet for a moment, she wondered what it would be like to have her own son or daughter someday.

"I haven't had a chance to meet your wife," Victoria Scarlett told Miguel. "Wendy mentioned that you had a small, intimate wedding last week. And that you flew to an island paradise for your honeymoon."

"This is Nicole Castleton...." Miguel paused for a beat before adding, "At least, she used to be. She's a Mendoza now."

Nicole set her bag on the floor, while still holding the painting, then reached out to greet each of the women. "It's nice to meet you. And I'm sorry that we weren't able to invite all of our family and friends to the wedding. It was such short notice that we thought it would be best to keep it small."

"That's what Wendy said. She also mentioned that Marcos is going to take her to that resort someday." Jordana shuffled little Jack to her other hip. "So tell me, how was your trip?"

"It was wonderful," Nicole said, afraid to glance at Miguel, afraid to see any sign of disagreement.

"It's so nice to see so many people getting married in Red Rock," Victoria said. "Two of my brothers are engaged, and my cousin Michael just got married."

Miguel reached for the bag Nicole had set on the ground. "We'd like to hang out here and talk more, but we're both exhausted and eager to get home."

Home. Was Miguel still planning to go to her house?

Nicole didn't think she could bear another night of being in the same room with Miguel again and not act on her impulses.

"Honey?" he said. "We'd better get out of here. Sawyer is probably waiting at the curb."

"Yes, of course. It was nice meeting you. We'll have to get together sometime soon."

"We'd like that," Jordana said.

After heading for the main entrance of the terminal, Nicole shielded her eyes from the sun. She might be tired, since she got very little sleep last night, but she wasn't the least bit eager to get home—or to have a discussion about what went on at Suenos del Sol—or more specifically, what hadn't gone on.

Avoiding confrontations came easily to her, especially after growing up with her father. So maybe she'd duck out on her own and give Miguel some time to unwind. Or even to hang out with his friend.

She blew out a sigh as she scanned the road, looking for her red Lexus, which Sawyer would be driving. "I know you mentioned being tired, Miguel, but if you don't mind, after Sawyer picks us up, I'd like to ask him to drop me off at the office. I can catch a ride home with a coworker. And that way, if you two want some time to…you know, grab a beer or something, you can do that."

"You want to go to the office on a Friday afternoon? I thought you weren't going in until Monday."

"I've been gone a long time. There are a lot of things I really need to take care of."

"Whatever you say. But why don't you drop us off wherever Sawyer left his Jag. Then you'll have your car."

"Okay, that would work."

But would it? Oh, no. Her heart cramped at the thought of what she'd just suggested. She could see Miguel and Sawyer now, two of the best-looking bachelors in Red Rock, having a beer and checking out single women. Not that she expected Miguel to do something like that until after their arrangement had ended. But who knew when that would be? After what happened on the beach…

She had no idea what Miguel planned to do now, but she assumed he'd tell her that he no longer wanted to go along with the ruse. And at this point, she really didn't blame him.

She'd known the marriage wouldn't last, but she hadn't realized it would end before it even started. And she wasn't sure what she'd tell her parents when her scheme completely unraveled.

But that seemed to be the least of her worries now.

Because she'd just set the scene for two of Red Rock's most eligible bachelors to take off in a fancy Jaguar convertible, looking for action....

Chapter Eleven

Nicole never wore casual skirts and blouses to the corporate office, but she did today. She also arrived wearing a cute pair of flip-flops she'd purchased in Santa Inez.

But going home to change into something more professional hadn't been an option. She'd been too eager to put some space between her and Miguel.

However, if she thought the atmosphere at home was going to be tense, it ended up being ten times worse at work—where she'd run to escape a confrontation with the man who'd turned her life on end, her new husband, only to find endless confrontations to avoid at Castleton Boots.

The tension started when Bradley came into her office carrying files, as if he intended to report on the goings on at Castleton Boots while she'd been away, but he'd plopped into the chair in front of her desk and wanted to know all about the resort and the amenities.

Apparently, he was planning a honeymoon of his own.

He'd no more than walked out of her office when her coworkers began to file in to congratulate her on her marriage.

It got to the point that she couldn't get any work done at all. But then again, that might have still been the case if she'd been left alone. Her mind was so taken up by thoughts of Miguel that she wouldn't have been able to get much done anyway.

Finally, at a quarter to four, she leaned over the paperwork on her desk, trying to focus on one of the reports Bradley had left with her, but not having much luck. It was next to impossible to be productive when her whole life was falling apart.

Maybe she ought to go home, although Miguel might have packed his bags by now. That is, if he and Sawyer weren't out on the town.

She could have talked things over with him on the plane, but she hadn't wanted Tanner to hear their conversation. And then, once they got into the car to head home…well, there was Sawyer to consider. And while he'd been sweet and charming, he'd reminded her so much of Miguel that his presence alone was enough to make her realize that she'd cast her ex-lover in a role that was completely out of character for a bachelor to fill.

"That's it," she uttered to herself, as she gathered

the paperwork together into a single pile. "I've got to get out of here."

Before she could scoot back her desk chair—or figure out just where she might go to escape this time—her father's voice sounded in the doorway. "I see you're back."

Nicole glanced over her shoulder and offered him a smile, trying to put up a front and act like a blissful newlywed. "Yes, we flew in early this afternoon."

Her dad studied her a moment, as though he was peeling away each and every lie she'd ever told him, removing the facade of her marriage.

Still, she'd try her best to put on a happy face, as well as a good show, in order to convince him that the honeymoon had been a romantic dream come true.

But what would happen if she went home, only to find Miguel and his belongings gone? She'd have to tell her father that his suspicions had been right all along, that she didn't really know Miguel at all.

What had possessed her to come up with the marriage-for-hire plan anyway? Why hadn't she taken Miguel's advice in New York? Why hadn't she just confronted her father and thrown down the gauntlet, telling him that she'd walk away from him, her mother and Castleton Boots before she'd allow him to force her into marriage?

Truthfully? Because she didn't think a confrontation like that would work with a man like her dad.

But now look at her. If Miguel ended their agreement, she stood to lose it all anyway.

"Nice outfit," her father said.

She glanced down at the summery skirt and blouse, then back at her dad. "Thank you."

"It's a little too casual for office wear."

So fire me, she wanted to say.

Instead, she gave a little shrug and turned her attention back to her papers.

After her father went home for the night, Nicole finally grabbed her purse, locked up the office and headed for the elevator.

She arrived at her condo at a quarter to six, parked in the garage and let herself into the kitchen, only to see Miguel standing at her stove and to catch a whiff of tomatoes, oregano and basil.

"What are you doing?" she asked, stunned to find that her assumptions about his whereabouts had been wrong.

Miguel glanced over his shoulder and flashed her a boyish grin. "Marcos isn't the only Mendoza brother who knows how to cook."

She stood like that for a moment, taking in the sight of her tall, dark and sexy husband-in-name-only moving about her kitchen.

Clearly, if he was still annoyed with her after their encounter at the beach, he didn't show it. On the contrary, he seemed happy to have her home.

"Listen," she said. "I owe you an apology. I'm sorry for sending you mixed messages at the beach. It's just that…well, the rum and the romantic setting were playing havoc with my better judgment. And I panicked."

"There wasn't anything 'mixed' about it. You wanted to make love as badly as I did. And just for the record, I still want to. But I won't force myself on you. You'll have to make the first move. And when you're ready, you know where to find me."

Where? she wondered. But she knew the answer to that. He'd made an agreement, a commitment, and he meant to keep it. He'd be *here*. With her until the end.

"By the way," Miguel said, "your Realtor called. The escrow closed on the house. All you have to do is let the movers know when you want them to come. They'll pack things up for you. You don't have to lift a finger to do a thing unless you want to."

Truthfully? Her heart wasn't into moving anymore, no matter how cute the new house was, no matter how far she wanted to get away from her parents. In fact, she didn't know what she wanted, other than the man standing in her kitchen.

"Dinner's almost ready," he said. "We can eat now or later."

The choice was hers, it seemed.

When to eat. When to move.

Isn't that what she'd wanted? To call the shots? To make all the decisions in her life?

But along with making those decisions came the responsibility for the consequences that followed.

"Just give me a minute to freshen up," she told Miguel.

And to figure out what was holding her back from taking full control of her life—and full responsibility for the consequences of her actions.

After a quiet dinner, Miguel and Nicole watched television in her living room for a while, but she turned in early, saying she was tired.

That might have been true, but he figured she had a lot on her mind. But he did, too.

He'd been so frustrated that last night at Suenos del Sol that he'd taken a cold shower. When he returned to the living room, Nicole was already on the sofa. Her eyes had been closed, but he'd suspected she'd only been pretending to be asleep, avoiding him and the situation they'd put themselves in.

He wished he could say that he was angry at her, that he blamed her for turning him on, then cutting him loose.

But he'd thought about it after he went to bed that night—and all the next day, during their flight back to Red Rock. In truth, he was angry at himself for agreeing to the crazy scheme of hers in the first place.

Like it or not, they both had some things to think about. As for him, he still had strong feelings for her, and he wanted to see if they could find some of what they'd once had.

But until she could stand up to her parents, particularly her father, he couldn't see much hope for them as a couple—a real one.

So apparently, that's where they were now.

Trouble was, he hadn't been kidding when he had said that he still wanted to make love with her—and badly. And he wasn't sure how much longer he could tolerate being so close to her without doing something about the attraction that only grew stronger each day and not waiting for her to make the first move.

As he turned over in bed, plumping and adjusting the pillow to make a comfortable spot for his head, a light rap sounded at the door, so light he questioned whether he'd actually heard it at all.

Then it happened again, louder this time.

"Come in," he said.

The knob turned, the door opened and Nicole walked in. She wore a white, lightweight nightgown. "Did I wake you?"

"No. Come on in." He sat up, the covers dropping to his lap. "What's up?"

"I'm sorry. I know it's late, but something's bothering me, and I've got to get it off my chest. I'm afraid it's driving me crazy, and it can't wait until morning."

He'd hoped that she was coming to tell him that she'd reconsidered, that she'd decided she wanted to make love after all, but she didn't seem to be struggling with passion or desire right now.

"What's wrong?" he asked.

The light in the hall silhouetted her form as she moved toward the bed, and he felt himself stir at the sight of her, at the tips of her nipples and the realization that she was naked under that flimsy gown.

"I'm going to let you out of the deal we made," she

said, taking a seat on the edge of the mattress. "You can keep the money, of course. But I can't continue pretending that we're married."

His gut clenched in spite of the freedom and the no-strings-attached cash she offered. "Why?"

"Because I can't continue living with you, pretending…"

An unexpected jolt of disappointment shook him to the core, because a part of him not only wanted the marriage to be real for the duration, but that he might even go so far as to admit that he liked the idea of it lasting…indefinitely.

So her unhappiness took him a moment to regroup. "You don't like being around me?"

Her eyes widened, and her lips parted. "No, that's not it at all. In fact, I like being around you way too much."

The disappointment faded away, and a slow grin spread across his face. "I don't see the problem in that."

"There's a huge problem in it, Miguel. I know all of this was my idea, but it was a bad one. I don't know what I was thinking when I suggested it. Marriage isn't a game."

She was right—all the way around. "So what are you suggesting?"

"I don't want to compound the mistakes I made in the past by enduring this crazy situation any longer. And quite frankly, I'm not sure why you don't hate me." Her gaze sought his, as if desperate to find an answer there. "You don't hate me, do you?"

At that, he couldn't help but chuckle. "You frustrate the hell out of me at times, but I don't hate you."

He supposed he could go on to admit that he still had feelings for her, but he also foresaw some bumps in the road ahead, and he wasn't ready to go out on a limb like that. So he opted to take the conversation in another direction.

"What mistakes did you make?" he asked.

"I'm afraid there are too many to count. But the biggest one was letting you go in the first place."

He'd been waiting ten years to hear her admit that, and he took a moment to savor the words—and more importantly, their meaning.

"If that's the case," he finally said, "then why are you doing it again?"

"Doing what?"

"Letting me go."

"I…" She bit down on her bottom lip, as if perplexed by what he was saying. Or was she struggling with what she was feeling?

Maybe that was it, because he certainly was. Making love was no longer the only issue. They were both tiptoeing around the emotional aspects of their "marriage."

When she finally looked up and caught his eye, their gazes met, then locked. Something powerful passed through them, then snaked around them, binding them fast and firm.

They remained like that for a moment, him sitting up under the sheets, her perched beside him on the edge of the bed.

Losing the battle to touch her—and unable to wait a moment longer—he reached under a silky skein of her hair and placed his hand at the nape of her neck. "Don't let go, honey. Not yet."

Then he drew her lips to his.

The kiss began sweetly, tenderly—like the first one they'd shared as innocent young lovers. Then it deepened, intensifying with the passion of maturity and the yearning of lost years, lost dreams.

Nicole skimmed her fingers across his chest, snagging a nipple with her nail and sending a ripple of heat through his veins.

Never in his life had Miguel wanted a woman the way he wanted Nicole. She did something to him when they were teens. And now, ten years later, nothing had changed, other than it had only gotten stronger.

He ran his hands along the curve of her back, rumpling the cotton of her gown. As he continued to caress, to explore her curves, to cup her breasts, she whimpered into his mouth, then arched forward, revealing her own need, her own arousal.

Miguel didn't have to ask her if she wanted to climb under the sheets with him, if she wanted to lie beside him, as naked as he was. He could feel it in her kiss, hear it in her sighs.

As if reading his mind, she rose to her feet long enough to remove her nightgown, baring herself to him.

She'd been lovely before, long and lean. But she'd filled out in a womanly way.

"You're more beautiful than I remembered, Nicole."

"So are you." She touched his shoulder, caressed it, then placed both hands on his chest and pushed him back down onto the mattress.

While he watched, she climbed up, leaning over him, her breasts almost within reach of his kiss.

Anticipation heightened his desire until he drew her down, feeling her breasts as they splayed upon his chest, her lips as they pressed against his.

He wasn't sure how long he could wait to be inside her. But they had all night, and he planned to use every minute of it.

As they lay together, he loved her with his hands, with his mouth until they were both wound tight with need.

He rolled to the side, taking her with him. "I've been wanting you, wanting this since…"

"…since the last time," she finished.

She was right.

He'd had sex before. More times than he could count. But it had never been like this.

As he entered her, she arched up, meeting him and beginning the dance they'd learned so many years ago. The beat and rhythm he'd never been able to repeat, other than in his memory.

With each thrust, her body responded to his. Time stood still, and nothing mattered but the two of them.

They reached a peak together, releasing in a cry and a shudder that had him seeing stars.

He had no idea what tomorrow would bring—a wallop of reality, no doubt—but right now, wrapped in Nicole's arms, he could almost believe in words like *love* and *forever*.

In the morning, as dawn stretched across the guestroom, Nicole woke up nestled in Miguel's arms.

Last night had been nothing short of magical, and while she'd nearly told him that she loved him several times, she'd managed to hold it back for fear that it was too soon, that it would scare him off.

But now, as she watched the gentle rise and fall of his chest, as she saw his eyes closed in slumber, she whispered the words she'd been wanting to say. "I love you."

Maybe someday in the very near future, she'd be brave enough to say them to him out loud.

Still, she wondered what the future held for them. She'd promised him a divorce once she was named CEO of Castleton Boots. Would he hold her to it? Or had making love changed all of that?

For the next ten minutes or so, Nicole cuddled in Miguel's arms. Then he began to stir.

"Good morning," she said.

"Mmm." He drew her closer, and nuzzled her neck.

She could get used to mornings like this, but nature called and she needed to run to the bathroom.

"How about some coffee?" she asked.

"Sounds good. But why don't you have someone else make it? I'd rather you stayed here, with me."

She laughed. "Maybe I should consider hiring a housekeeper to make coffee for us tomorrow."

"Maybe so."

Well, the implication was that there'd be more nights like the one they'd just spent. So that was good, wasn't it?

She pressed a kiss on his cheek, then slipped out of bed and padded to the bathroom. After a quick shower, she went into her bedroom and dressed for the day. Then she headed to the kitchen and put on a pot of coffee.

While it brewed, she pulled out a container of orange juice, a carton of eggs and a loaf of bread. Then she set about fixing breakfast.

Ten minutes later, Miguel joined her, his hair damp from the shower. He wore a pair of jeans and a T-shirt, and she wondered if he planned to hang out at the house or if he was going to check on the building. She suspected he'd want to see how much work Roberto had gotten done this past week.

"I hate to put a damper on things," Miguel said, "but I'd like you to have a talk with your parents."

"About what?"

He poured himself a glass of orange juice, then leaned against the counter. "About our marriage."

"What about it?"

"I want you to tell them the truth."

Her tummy tossed and lurched. "Even if it means that I'd have to sacrifice Castleton Boots?"

"First off, I don't think you'd lose the company."

"But I very well could. So why take the chance?"

"Because, if you can't level with them, then you're playing games—with them and with me."

She crossed her arms and lifted her chin. "I'm not playing games with you."

"How can I be sure that you won't someday? For some reason, you're afraid to challenge your parents, especially your dad. And it's easier for you to go behind his back. What kind of relationship is that?"

The only one she knew. Besides, what kind of relationship did she and Miguel have? She'd be damned if she knew. And he wasn't talking.

So ask him, a small voice urged.

Yeah, right. And have him remind her of their business deal? Have him tell her that he's going to use the money to open a nightclub, to be out every night, especially on Fridays and Saturdays?

The ultimate bachelor had certainly chosen the perfect career.

"My relationship with my parents is none of your business."

Miguel crossed his arms. "Your reluctance to confront them when they're wrong or intruding in your life is proof that you've never grown up. You might dress like a twenty-six-year-old executive, but you're still that sixteen-year-old girl hoping Daddy will buy her a car if she studies hard and gets good grades."

Nicole wanted to scream. To cry. To shake her fists and order Miguel out of her house.

Instead she squared her shoulders, determined to put some distance between them while she wrapped her mind around his accusations—especially since she had to admit there might be more than a bit of truth to them.

"You know," she said, scanning the kitchen in search of her purse and spotting it near the telephone, "I hate to cut this conversation short, but I've got to go to the office for a couple hours."

"It's Saturday. I think you're just making an excuse to avoid confronting me, too."

She hated that he was right. And that he knew that she knew.

"Then I guess I have some soul searching to do," she said, as she snatched her purse and prepared to leave the house.

"So do I."

Then he walked out, beating her to it.

Chapter Twelve

After Miguel had left the condo and the front door had snapped shut behind him, Nicole paced the kitchen floor.

She stopped long enough to rake her fingers through the top strands of her hair and tried to sort the truth from the lies.

Bottom line? She loved Miguel—and probably always had. But it seemed easier to let him go than to admit to him just how much he meant to her, only to risk learning that his love for her had died years ago. And that what she'd seen or thought she'd seen in his eyes had only been an illusion, something she'd dreamed up.

It would kill her to watch him walk away with a spring in his step, a copy of the divorce decree in his hand and her personal check in his wallet.

But he was asking her to man up—or woman up, if you will—and go to her parents, to admit that she'd deceived them.

For some reason, you're afraid to challenge your parents, especially your dad. And it's easier for you to go behind his back.

He'd been right. She never had liked going head-to-head with her father, when she knew going in to either the boardroom or his study that she'd ultimately lose.

But hadn't she lost already?

She'd certainly lost Miguel when she'd been younger. She'd even lost bits and pieces of herself over the years each time she rolled over, swallowed her pride or went with the flow.

You might dress like a twenty-six-year-old executive, Miguel had said, *but you're still that sixteen-year-old girl hoping Daddy will buy her a car if she studies hard and gets good grades.*

Nicole had wanted to argue, to tell him he was wrong. But the truth had stunned her into realizing who she'd become, both inside and out.

Sure she had a closet full of fashionable clothes suitable for a woman of her social status. Yet while she actually enjoyed dressing for success, there were days when she would have liked going into the office in a pair of comfortable old jeans, dressed up by a stylish pair of Castleton Boots. But her father had insisted that she had to look the part of a corporate exec if she wanted people to take her seriously.

Most people did.

It was her father who didn't.

So she'd gone along with his request, telling herself that when she became the CEO, she'd ease up on the office dress code.

But now that the whole marriage scheme had fallen apart, it wasn't a question of *when* she'd become the CEO but *if.*

The way she saw it, she had two options. She could either tell her parents the truth about the marriage deception or Miguel would walk out on their deal. But if he did that, she'd be forced to admit that her father had been right all along, that she hadn't known Miguel well enough. And for that reason, their renewed romance hadn't lasted much longer than the weeklong honeymoon.

The more she thought about it, the angrier she got—at her father for being so unreasonable and controlling. And at Miguel for having the audacity to issue an ultimatum like he'd just done. In doing so, he'd treated her like a child, just as he'd accused her father of doing.

But she was also angry at herself for not taking control of her own life earlier. And for letting the two men she loved most in the world think they could use her love for them to force her hand. It might have worked in the past, but it wouldn't happen again.

From this day forward, Nicole would think and speak for herself. And if things went down badly, today or in the future, at least it would be on her own terms.

With that decided, she grabbed her purse off the counter and reached inside for her keys. Then she went out into the garage and climbed into her car. It was time to visit her parents and to let them know that she wasn't a little girl anymore.

Minutes later, she parked in front of her parents' estate. In the past, she might have waited for a moment, bolstering her courage, pondering her speech. But not today.

She made her way to the front door with a determined step. She might lose Miguel and the company, but she'd be damned if she'd lose any more of herself.

When she reached the front door, she rang the bell, then let herself in. "Mom? Dad? It's me."

Her mother entered the marble-tiled foyer first, wearing neatly pressed black slacks, a cream-colored silk blouse and a smile. "Hi, honey. What a nice surprise."

Nicole had no time for small talk. "Mom, I need to talk to you and Daddy. Is he here?"

Before her mother could respond, her father spoke from the top of the circular staircase. "Yes, I'm here. What's wrong?"

Nicole squared her shoulders. "I have a confession to make, and I think it's best if you both sit down."

"Oh, for goodness' sake," Mom said. "I knew it. I didn't want to ask you before, but I suspected it all along. You're pregnant. That's the reason for the quick wedding, isn't it?"

"Well, at least they made it legal," her father said, as he made his way downstairs. "And she's not showing. We can be thankful for that."

"Relax," Nicole said, crossing her arms and bracing herself for the showdown. "I'm not pregnant. But I have to admit, I'm a little surprised by your reactions. After all, you were so eager to become grandparents that you forced me into marriage."

"We did no such thing," her mother said.

"Actually," Nicole corrected, "you backed me into a corner. But that's my fault."

"What are you talking about?" her father asked.

Okay, so they wanted the explanation before gathering in the living room and taking a seat. She could deal with that. They'd just have the showdown here in the foyer.

Nicole shifted her weight to one hip. "After learning that I had to be married to take control of the company, I went looking for Miguel. And I paid him to marry me."

Her mother gasped. "I can't believe you'd stoop to something so low."

"Now just wait one minute." Nicole raised her index finger and pointed it at them both. "You were the ones who made the first 'stoop.' I just responded in a knee-jerk reaction. And you were right, Daddy. Miguel and I were young before. And we really didn't know each other as adults. But over the course of what began as a marriage of convenience, I realized that what had started out as a sham became real for me. I still love Miguel—with all my heart and soul."

"How does he feel about you?" Mom asked.

Nicole wished she could say that he felt the same way, but she wasn't sure. He had once upon a time. Did he still?

Yet even if he did, she had no idea how he'd feel, how he'd react after she let him have it. Because the confrontation with her father wasn't the only one she meant to have today.

Either way, while she was tempted to continue the facade and take the easy way out, she wouldn't.

No more lies and half-truths. And no more avoidance.

"I'm not sure how Miguel feels," she admitted. "I think he loves me. I hope so. Either way, I'm going to try and make a go of our marriage. And I came here to tell you that you'll either accept Miguel with open arms— just as his family has accepted me—or you won't be seeing very much of me in the future."

"You don't have to threaten us," Dad said. "Your mother and I were only trying to look out for you. But to tell you the truth, Nicole, I'm not convinced that the Mendoza kid loves you. After all, you told me yourself that you offered him money to marry you. And he accepted it, didn't he? That just goes to show you what kind of man he is."

"Miguel can't be bought. He turned me down flat the first time I asked him. I had to beg him and remind him of a promise he once made. He's an honorable man, Dad."

Her father let out a "Humph," then added, "Need I remind you how much money our family has? He stands to be very wealthy if he sticks by you, even if it's just for a couple years."

Ouch. At this point, the old Nicole might have backed

down, might have slumped her shoulders, clamped her mouth shut.

But not the new Nicole.

"I'm not going to say it again, Dad. You and Mom will accept Miguel and our marriage. And if you don't, I'll walk away from Castleton Boots. Because you were right—a life that's all about work is no life at all. If I have to start over from scratch, I will. But I'll be starting over with Miguel—if he'll have me."

It was a bold stand, but one she was willing to make. Besides, she had to admit that her mom and dad might have been right about her priorities. She did need to reconsider the things she found most important in life.

"Nicole," her father began, "don't get your dander up. I'll have my attorney draft a new document first thing Monday morning. I'll be handing over the reins to you and cutting out the marriage stipulation. No matter what you and Miguel decide, your mother and I will accept him. It'll just take a little time for me to get used to, that's all."

"What's there to get used to?"

He shrugged. "I don't know. It's been hard enough seeing you grow up and make a life of your own. Knowing that there's another man taking my place, well, that won't be easy."

She blew out a sigh, confused at his faulty logic. "Then why did you insist upon me getting married?"

"That was your mother's doing. She's the one who wanted to see you happy and with a family before she died. And I just…well, I went along with it."

Nicole shot a glance at her mom, who managed a wistful smile. "Would it be okay with you if I planned a small wedding reception for you and Miguel? I'd always dreamed of... Well, everything happened so fast."

"I'll have to talk it over with Miguel," she said. But if he intended to go through with a divorce, there wouldn't be anything to celebrate.

"By the way," her dad said, "tell that young man that I'll even give him a position in the company."

That was quite an admission, coming from Andy Castleton. And it pleased her to be able to say, "Miguel won't take it, Dad. He'd never be happy working for Castleton Boots. Besides, he's got his heart set on opening a nightclub."

And now that she'd gotten things settled with her parents, she wondered if there was anything else Miguel might have his heart set on.

What a jerk.

Miguel had driven around town aimlessly for the past fifteen minutes, only to come to the conclusion that he'd been way out of line. What in creation had compelled him to provoke a fight with Nicole *this* morning—of all mornings?

He'd just spent the most amazing night in her arms, reliving sweet memories and making new ones. And then dawn rolled around. He hadn't needed to ask her if the sex had been good for her. He'd known beyond all doubt that it had been better than either one of them had remembered or dreamed of.

There was, of course, the other standard question that usually followed a couple's first night of lovemaking: *Now what?*

He should have told her how he felt, what he hoped the future would bring. Instead, he'd let past hurts and disappointments run away with him, and he'd made a complete mess of everything.

Trouble was, he'd been carrying a chip on his shoulder ever since her dad told her to break up with him— and she'd gone along with that order. And that anger had festered over the years.

So when he started thinking about his feelings for her, about wanting to give their marriage a chance, he realized the only thing that had come between them in the past had been her father. And that as long as she was reluctant to stand up to the man, then Miguel would never be a priority in her life.

And he refused to come in second to her daddy.

At that point, he had to know if she could break free of the hold Andy had on her, as well as the need to please him no matter what. And so Miguel had thrown down the gauntlet, so to speak, testing the waters. Testing her.

When she had grabbed her purse, planning to walk away rather than even talking about it, he'd lost it and left before she had the chance to.

Still, he shouldn't have said the things he did. And after coming to grips with the fact that he owed her an apology, if not a heartfelt confession, he'd driven back to her house.

Only now that he was here, she was gone. And he couldn't tell her what he should have said earlier.

But what should he have told her? That he loved her? That he always had, always would?

Hell, he wasn't sure where a profession like that would lead, especially now that he'd stirred everything up.

But the truth was, he wanted more than a business deal with Nicole. He wanted the real deal. And if that meant courting her and dating her…

Then that's what he'd have to do.

And if she broke his heart all over again, then that was a risk he'd have to take—assuming that she didn't want to end it all right now, especially after the can of worms he'd opened this morning.

He'd no more than taken a seat in her living room when the doorknob clicked and the door swung open.

He turned, glad it was her—until he saw the fire in her eye. He meant to apologize—he *really* did.

But before he could get a word out, she lifted her index finger and pointed it at him like a schoolmarm on a mission. "I have a few words to say to you. First of all, don't ever issue an ultimatum like that to me again. You treated me no differently than my father does—or rather than he used to. And I won't stand for it anymore."

Miguel hadn't realized his comments had come across that way, but before he could utter either an apology or a response, she added, "You had a point, though. And for that reason alone, I drove over to talk to my parents. I told them that our marriage was a sham. And that I would walk away from Castleton Boots before I'd let them force me into doing something I didn't want to do."

Bravo. But was she going to lower her finger? Or give him an opportunity to speak?

"I also need to thank you," she added.

Did he dare ask why?

"First of all, it felt really good to stand up for myself. So while you were completely out of line, you actually did me a favor. And secondly, you were right. When I told my father he could have the company, that I didn't want it if it meant I had to sell myself short, he did roll over. On Monday morning, he's going to have his attorney draw up new documents that make me his successor. I'm going to be the new CEO of Castleton Boots."

"That's great news." Of course, that meant she wouldn't need a husband anymore. And while disappointment clouded his hope, it didn't change the facts or his pride. "I'm happy for you, Nicole. You deserve the position, as well as his respect."

"Thank you. I appreciate that. But that's not all I have to say. I also have a question for you. And I want an honest answer."

"Okay. Shoot."

She took a deep breath, then slowly let it out. "How do you feel about all of this?"

"All of what?"

"Our marriage. Do you still want a divorce?"

She was giving him a choice? Did that mean that ending things wasn't a slam dunk?

"What do *you* want?" he asked.

"I'd like to make a go of it, for real. And while you implied that if I told my parents the truth about it only being a marriage of convenience, that you'd stick around…" Up went the schoolmarm's finger again. "And just so you know, that's *not* why I talked to them. Anyway, I wasn't sure if the ultimatum you gave me was only an excuse to break up sooner. Or if you actually meant what you said and that you wanted to…you know, stay married?"

A grin stretched across Miguel's face. "Now I'm the one with an apology to make."

She arched a brow. "For being a jerk?"

"You took the words right out of my mouth. I was way out of line, honey. I should have told you how amazing it was to make love with you last night. I should have helped you fix breakfast and do the dishes. And all the while we should have talked about feelings and the future. But for some reason, I was running scared."

"Of what?"

"Of you, of us. Of reaching for a dream, only to lose it all over again."

"I'm not following you. Are you talking about the nightclub?"

"No, honey. The biggest dream I ever had was *you.* I may have told myself that somewhere along the way I got over you, but I was lying to myself. And with each day we spent together, I grew to love you more. And somewhere deep inside, I hoped…I *believed* that if I went along with your marriage scheme, that I could make you fall in love with me all over again."

Nicole slowly shook her head, a smile forming. "I didn't need to fall in love with you again, Miguel. I never stopped. Like you, I convinced myself that those feelings had died. But they were way too strong for that. And so that's why I could never get serious with anyone else. I compared every man I met with you and always found him lacking."

"And that's why I never settled down, either. And why I could never commit to anyone else."

"So what about now?" she asked. "Are you ready to commit to me, to make this thing real?"

"In a heartbeat."

Then he took her in his arms and kissed her with all the love he'd stored in his heart over the years, all the dreams they'd ever had, all the promises they'd ever uttered.

Just as they came up for a breather, the telephone rang and Nicole answered.

"Hi, Mom." She listened a while, then said, "Why don't I let you talk to Miguel."

Now what? he wondered.

Nicole covered the mouthpiece, and as she handed the phone to him, she lowered her voice. "My mom and dad want us to come to dinner tonight—or any night we're free. They want to start things off on a better foot—at home, where it'll be more relaxed and comfortable."

At their home, and not the country club? Miguel had

to admit he wouldn't mind having a chance to meet with them again.

So when Elizabeth Castleton issued the invitation to him, they agreed upon having dinner tonight at six.

"By the way," Miguel said to the woman on the line, "I know that Nicole and I are already married, technically. But under the circumstances, I'd like to say those vows over again, next time in a church ceremony for everyone to see. I'm not sure how you and Mr. Castleton feel about that, but it would be nice to have your support."

"We'd love to help in any way we can. And please, call us Andy and Elizabeth—or even Mom and Dad, if you'd rather."

He could handle first names, although anything more intimate than that would be pushing it at this point.

"All right," he said. "We'll see you at six."

"Good. We can talk more about wedding plans then."

"I'm looking forward to it."

Miguel passed the telephone to Nicole so she could say goodbye, then she disconnected the line.

"That was really sweet of you. My mom had always dreamed of me having a big wedding. And she'd really wanted to see me get married in a church."

"I'm not doing it for her. I'm doing it for us. But if it makes her happy, that's a plus."

As Nicole slipped her arms around his waist, ready for another kiss, it seemed, he tossed out another question. "I don't suppose you'd consider selling both the condo and the new house so we could purchase a home together. One that would be located closer to the night-club."

She smiled, her eyes brightening. "We can live in an apartment or a trailer if it brings you closer to your dreams."

"My dreams came true the day you walked into my office in New York and asked me to marry you."

"I'm just glad you went along with my crazy scheme."

"I have to admit, I only went along with it because seeing you again turned my heart every which way but loose. And I couldn't imagine letting you go back to Red Rock alone."

"You have no idea how happy I am that you took me up on that offer."

"I'll bet I do know." He brushed a kiss across her lips. "But promise me something."

"Anything."

"From now on, no more games, okay? I want our marriage to be based on love, honesty and trust."

"I promise you that, from this day on."

"For better or worse?" he asked.

Nicole kissed him. "And for as long as we both shall live."

* * * * *

Look for the next installment in the new
Special Edition continuity
THE FORTUNES OF TEXAS:
SOUTHERN INVASION
After a one-night stand on New Year's Eve,
Shane Fortune went back to Atlanta and focused his
attention on settling family business. Now he's re-
turned to Red Rock to find a big surprise in a very
small package—he's going to be a daddy!

Don't miss
EXPECTING FORTUNE'S HEIR
by Cindy Kirk

On sale May 2013,
wherever Harlequin Books are sold.

REQUEST YOUR FREE BOOKS!

2 FREE NOVELS PLUS 2 FREE GIFTS!

♥ HARLEQUIN®

SPECIAL EDITION

Life, Love & Family

YES! Please send me 2 FREE Harlequin® Special Edition novels and my 2 FREE gifts (gifts are worth about $10). After receiving them, if I don't wish to receive any more books, I can return the shipping statement marked "cancel." If I don't cancel, I will receive 6 brand-new novels every month and be billed just $4.49 per book in the U.S. or $5.24 per book in Canada. That's a savings of at least 14% off the cover price! It's quite a bargain! Shipping and handling is just 50¢ per book in the U.S. and 75¢ per book in Canada.* I understand that accepting the 2 free books and gifts places me under no obligation to buy anything. I can always return a shipment and cancel at any time. Even if I never buy another book, the two free books and gifts are mine to keep forever.

235/335 HDN FVTV

Name	(PLEASE PRINT)

Address		Apt. #

City	State/Prov.	Zip/Postal Code

Signature (if under 18, a parent or guardian must sign)

Mail to the **Harlequin® Reader Service:**
IN U.S.A.: P.O. Box 1867, Buffalo, NY 14240-1867
IN CANADA: P.O. Box 609, Fort Erie, Ontario L2A 5X3

Want to try two free books from another line?
Call 1-800-873-8635 or visit www.ReaderService.com.

* Terms and prices subject to change without notice. Prices do not include applicable taxes. Sales tax applicable in N.Y. Canadian residents will be charged applicable taxes. Offer not valid in Quebec. This offer is limited to one order per household. Not valid for current subscribers to Harlequin Special Edition books. All orders subject to credit approval. Credit or debit balances in a customer's account(s) may be offset by any other outstanding balance owed by or to the customer. Please allow 4 to 6 weeks for delivery. Offer available while quantities last.

Your Privacy—The Harlequin® Reader Service is committed to protecting your privacy. Our Privacy Policy is available online at www.ReaderService.com or upon request from the Harlequin Reader Service.

We make a portion of our mailing list available to reputable third parties that offer products we believe may interest you. If you prefer that we not exchange your name with third parties, or if you wish to clarify or modify your communication preferences, please visit us at www.ReaderService.com/consumerschoice or write to us at Harlequin Reader Service Preference Service, P.O. Box 9062, Buffalo, NY 14269. Include your complete name and address.

HSE13

SPECIAL EXCERPT FROM

H HARLEQUIN®

SPECIAL EDITION

USA TODAY *bestselling author Allison Leigh
brings us a sneak peek of A WEAVER VOW,
a new tale of love, loss and second chances in her*
RETURN TO THE DOUBLE-C *miniseries for
Harlequin® Special Edition®.*

***

Murphy, please don't get into more trouble.

Whatever had made her think she could be a better parent to Murphy than his other options? He needed a man around, not just a woman he could barely tolerate.

He needed his father.

And now all they had was each other.

Isabella Lockhart couldn't bear to think about it.

"It was an accident!" Murphy yelled. "Dude! That's my bat. You can't just take my bat!"

"I just did, *dude,*" the man returned flatly. He closed his hand over Murphy's thin shoulder and forcibly moved him away from Isabella.

Isabella rounded on the man, gaping at him. He was wearing a faded brown ball cap and aviator sunglasses that hid his eyes. "Take your hand off him! Who do you think you are?"

"The man your boy decided to aim at with his blasted baseball." His jaw was sharp and shadowed by brown stubble and his lips were thinned.

"I did not!" Murphy screamed right into Isabella's ear.

She winced, then pointed. "Go sit down."

She drew in a calming breath and turned her head into the breeze that she'd begun to suspect never died here in Weaver, Wyoming, before facing the man again. "I'm Isabella Lockhart," she began.

"I know who you are."

She'd been in Weaver only a few weeks, but it really was a small town if people she'd never met already knew who she was.

"I'm sure we can resolve whatever's happened here, Mr. uh—?"

"Erik Clay."

Focusing on the woman in front of him was a lot safer than focusing on the skinny black-haired hellion sprawled on Ruby's bench.

She tucked her white-blond hair behind her ear with a visibly shaking hand. Bleached blond, he figured, considering the eyes that she turned toward the back of his truck were such a dark brown they were nearly black.

Even angry as he was, he wasn't blind to the whole effect.

Weaver's newcomer was a serious looker.

***

Don't miss A WEAVER VOW
by USA TODAY bestselling author Allison Leigh.

Available in May 2013 from
Harlequin® Special Edition® wherever books are sold.

EXPECTING FORTUNE'S HEIR
by Cindy Kirk

Shane Fortune is accustomed to women using his
family for money, so when the cute and spunky
Lia Serrano tells him that she is pregnant with his
baby after a one-night stand, he is seriously skeptical.
But after spending more time together, he can't help
but hope the baby is truly his....

Look for the next book in
The Fortunes of Texas:
Southern Invasion

Available in May from Harlequin Special Edition,
wherever books are sold.